PRAISE F

THE SHADOW OF UKUPACHA

A HARRY BAUER THRILLER

BLAKE BANNER

RIGHTHOUSE

ISBN-13: 978-1-63696-320-4

ISBN-10: 1-63696-320-X

Cover design by: Damonza

Printed in the United States of America

www.righthouse.com

www.instagram.com/righthousebooks

www.facebook.com/righthousebooks

twitter.com/righthousebooks

HARRY BAUER THRILLER SERIES
Dead of Night (Book 1)
Dying Breath (Book 2)
The Einstaat Brief (Book 3)
Quantum Kill (Book 4)
Immortal Hate (Book 5)
The Silent Blade (Book 6)
LA: Wild Justice (Book 7)
Breath of Hell (Book 8)
Invisible Evil (Book 9)
The Shadow of Ukupacha (Book 10)
Sweet Razor Cut (Book 11)
Blood of the Innocent (Book 12)
Blood on Balthazar (Book 13)
Simple Kill (Book 14)
Riding The Devil (Book 15)
The Unavenged (Book 16)
The Devil's Vengeance (Book 17)
Bloody Retribution (Book 18)
Rogue Kill (Book 19)
Blood for Blood (Book 20)

ONE

I WAS IN DC BECAUSE SENATOR RANDY ORTEGA HAD told the brigadier he wanted to discuss a "sensitive issue." When a senator tells the head of COBRA that he wants to discuss a "sensitive issue," it means there's somebody he wants eliminated. That's what COBRA does, it eliminates people who commit crimes against humanity, but are beyond the reach of the law. What was unusual, though, was that he had asked me to come along too. Usually the client uses the brigadier and the colonel to mediate. That way they don't get their hands dirty by associating with the executioner.

That's me, the executioner.

Senator Ortega's office was in the Old House Office Building, a name that belied the understated elegance and grandeur of the edifice on Independence Avenue, in the United States Capitol Complex. I arrived by cab and met the brigadier among marble echoes in the rotunda. He greeted me with a nod and we walked together without speaking, down the left-hand passage and around the dogleg, to the senator's office. There we entered the antechamber, guarded by his secretary. She had a mouth like a razorblade and blue eyes that doubled as stabbing instruments.

She was a living paradox in that she displaced her body from one location to another, while taking care not to move any part of it.

"The senator is expecting you, brigadier," she said, as though it were a grievous accusation, "go right on in." She pressed a button and the door buzzed and clunked softly. The brigadier pushed it open and we went inside. The door clunked behind us.

The office was large and had broad windows overlooking First Street. The floor was carpeted in royal blue, the furniture was all dark mahogany and oak, the walls were partially paneled in paler oak, and burgundy leather armchairs and a sofa occupied the space before an open fireplace. The senator was behind the desk, and behind him was the flag of the Unites States, and a photograph of the president, whom he did not support.

He stood as we entered and gave a comfortable laugh as he reached out for the brigadier's hand.

"Buddy! Good to see you. How've you been?" He grabbed the brigadier's hand with both of his own and pumped it, then looked at me and grinned.

"Harry! You mind if I call you Harry?"

We shook and I smiled. "It's preferable to what a lot of other people call me."

He gave a little jump when he laughed. He laughed loud, staring at the brigadier and then back at me.

"Those who are still alive, huh? Huh?" He laughed again, and feinted a punch at my chest. "You know what we call you 'round here? Those of us who know? We call you the 'H-bomb.' The H-bomb! Huh?"

The brigadier made for a chair with an unamused rictus on his face.

"I'd rather you didn't talk about him at all, Randy. Black coffee, please."

Randy shrugged and spread his hands. "I know, I know. It's just the few of us in the know. The H-bomb, it's good." He returned behind his desk and pressed a button. "Hey, Melinda, coffee for three, black. Sit."

This last was directed at me. The brigadier had already sat. I lowered myself into a comfortable leather armchair and he dropped into a black leather swivel chair that was probably big enough for his whole family to share.

I was getting bored with the polite preambles so I interrupted whatever it was he was about to say.

"Senator, it is extremely unusual for me, or any man in my position, to be invited to a meeting. Why am I here?"

He looked at me from under his eyebrows. "Talks like he shoots, huh? Straight to the point."

"Time is the one thing we can't restock."

He nodded like he agreed. "I don't know if you know much about me," he gestured at the brigadier with both hands, "or if Buddy has told you about my special interests...?"

"I know you were involved with the UFO disclosure movement. I'm afraid it's an issue that doesn't interest me much, so that's about all I do know." He hesitated a moment and I frowned and added, "If that is relevant here, I think maybe you have the wrong man."

He glanced at the brigadier who remained silent, then looked back at me.

"Don't worry, I'm not going to send you off to assassinate Paul." I arched an eyebrow which said I had no idea what he was talking about. He said, "Paul? The movie? No? Forget it. Listen, I am in Harry Reid's gang, but I'm definitely not into tinfoil hats and all that shit. I am briefed by the UAPTF and other very serious agencies, and I also have a special interest in what we might call the History of the American People. The way I see it, the fockin' Europeans..."

He paused with his mouth sagging open and grinned at the brigadier. "Sorry, Buddy, but you're not European anymore, right?"

"Right."

"Good, so the fockin' Europeans want a fockin' monopoly over history, because that makes them more fockin' civilized. You know what I'm sayin'? Man first appears in Africa, then moves into Europe and becomes super-advanced, democratic, technological, yadda yadda, and then, and only then, moves to the so-called 'New World.' Bullshit! Bull-shit! I got news for you—not for you, but for them. We were building pyramids and cities in America, with super-advanced technologies, when in Europe they were still learning to make huts out of wattle and daub. You know what I'm saying?"

"Sure, but I still don't get what this has to do with me. You want me to take out all the European historians?"

"I'm getting there. You have somewhere you need to be?" I made the face of patience and shook my head once. "So chill. And by the way," he grinned, "that wouldn't be a bad idea at all."

The door opened and Melinda came in, managing to walk and carry a tray while still not moving. She set the tray down on the desk and left.

"Enjoy the coffee and relax. This is about blood." He picked up his cup and sipped. "You guys, your ancestors come from Europe," he gestured at the brigadier, "not him. He comes from Britain, the smallest continent on Earth, but for us Latinos, with Indian blood, having our past robbed from us hurts. A lot of my constituents are Mexican, I got others from Colombia, Peru, and some Native North Americans too. And we feel that history is being deliberately manipulated to hide what was going on in America in ancient prehistory."

I sipped my coffee. He went on.

"So, I was active, and instrumental, in persuading the American Indian Studies Department of the University of Arizona to fund a dig in Peru, just outside San Julian, in the Convención province, in the region of Cusco. The dig is being supervised by a constituent of mine, who also happens to be a close friend, Dr. Elizabeth Caldwell. And I am here to tell you, pal, what they are digging up there, in the mountains above the Urubamba River, will blow your mind. I mean really blow your mind."

He watched for a response and got none, so he pressed on.

"OK, so at the same time, in the same town of San Julian, while Liz is up Mount Apusupay making the discovery that will turn our whole understanding of human history on its head, deep in the San Julian Valley, at the bottom of the San Julian Gorge, in dense rainforest, Dr. Amanda Epstein is conducting revolutionary, and highly secret, biochemical research on behalf of the Pasqüal Pharmaceutical Company of Munich. And before you ask, I have no idea what they are doing there."

I placed my empty cup on his desk and said, "OK, Senator, you have set the scene. Now, please, how do I fit into all this?"

He scowled at me a moment. "I thought you ninja guys were supposed to have infinite patience."

"I am not a ninja. I was with the British SAS and we tended to get things done fast and with a minimum of fuss and distraction."

"OK, Harry, just relax, everything I am telling you is relevant."

He pulled open a drawer in his desk and took out a transparent, plastic wallet. Inside it was a plain white envelope with a handwritten address on it in red ink. Beside that was a single sheet of paper. At a glance I could see it was also handwritten, all in caps and, oddly, in various different-colored inks.

The senator reached in the drawer again and removed three pairs of latex gloves from a pack. He tossed one pair to the brigadier and another to me. Then he pulled on his own pair and removed the contents from the transparent sheath. He slid the envelope across the desk to me.

"What do you make of that? The stamp and postmark are from Cusco, Peru. Sent two weeks ago. The address is written in capitals, in red ink, and despite the capitalization, personally, I think you can make out a childish, unformed hand."

"The use of red ink is also odd," I said.

"Yeah, I want to come back to that. See the letter?" He slipped it in front of me. "I'm going to give you a copy to take away with you. He uses four different colors of ink: blue, black, red and green. Here he switches in the middle of the paragraph. I don't know, maybe he was running out of ink. There seems to be no reason for the switches. He's not emphasizing anything. It seems to be random, but I think he was trying to tell me something. Something specific."

I picked it up and started to read it. I spoke as I read. "Like what? Color coding the information? Trying to draw your attention to certain paragraphs? Seems a complicated and unreliable way of doing it."

"Read it, then we'll talk about the ink."

I read:

DEAR SENATOR ORTEGA,

I am writing to you because I know how important American Indian history is for you. And I know that you have invested a lot of time and effort in making this excavation happen. But you should know that this is not the Golden Opportunity you thought. Some very bad things are happening here. People are dying. People are being taken into slavery. Women and children. People are having their souls sucked out and eaten by daemons.

There is awful evil at work here, Senator, and somebody has to look into it and do something about it. Danny tried talking to the alcalde and to the police in Cusco, but they said he was crazy. I have been warned to be quiet too, or I will die like Danny, or worse.

Please, Senator Ortega, do something. Danny tried and Danny died. Supay is coming in the tunnels and the deep caves, Senator, coming up from Ukupacha, and they will eat our souls. They will poison us first, with nuna miyu, and then they will eat our souls. They will eat all our souls, until no man and no woman on Earth is left with his soul.

Danny tried to warn, but Danny died. Soon we will all be living in death.

Look for me, I will show you.

Carl Allen

. . .

I LAID the letter down and looked into the senator's eyes. "OK, so you are taking this guy seriously and I wonder why. He is probably psychotic, or he is perpetrating a hoax. So what is making you give credence to what he is saying?"

He pointed at me. "That, see? That is the right question. And the answer is, there are two reasons. One, this guy is not crazy."

"You know him?"

"No, but he knows me. This is strictly between us. When I was much younger, I was a conspiracy nut, and I got involved in an investigation into an alleged experiment conducted by the US Navy involving Einstein's unified field theory, and a lot of weird shit that went down toward the end of the war. Anyhow, the whistle blower in that case, who tried to blow the lid off the experiments, was called Carl Allen. Now, Carl Allen wrote several letters to one Morris Jessup, in exactly this way: by hand and in various different-colored inks. The letters read like he was a schizophrenic, but much of what he said turned out..." He paused. "Well, never mind. The point is nobody knows anymore that I was involved in that investigation. But this Carl Allen clearly does. And in writing the letter in this way, he is telling me that this is an issue of similar importance."

"You investigated that experiment alone?"

"No, there were a couple of other people involved. They have all moved on and occupy positions in society."

I arched an eyebrow at him. "Any of them have kids who are studying archeology?"

"We all swore each other to secrecy."

I shook my head. "An oath of secrecy is as solid as the last glass of wine you drank. Kids meet in college, 'You'll never guess, I heard my dad telling a friend last night Senator Ortega used to be a UFO nut.' You may find all this compelling, Senator, but I'm afraid I don't."

"I didn't think you would, Harry. But the second reason will carry more weight with you. I made," he hesitated, "uh, discreet inquiries, through Liz, and she did have a boy working for her on the dig, a graduate student from Arizona, whose name was Danny Cooper. He became depressed about six months ago, climbed to the top of the Apusupay Mountain and threw himself off, into the Urubamba River."

"Danny Cooper? He wouldn't be any relation to Edwin Cooper, the Aerospace billionaire?"

He grunted and sighed. He delivered his answer to the brigadier. "He is like you described him." To me he said, "OK, so you do your homework. Good. Yeah, Ed was a friend of mine back in the day..."

"And like you he still has an interest in all things outer space. Wasn't he awarded a contract by the Air Force to carry out research into the ion drive recently?"

"Yes."

"So is he any relation to Danny Cooper."

"Ed is Danny's father. So I have a personal interest in this. Danny was almost a nephew to me."

I turned to look at the brigadier. He avoided my eye and gazed out of the window. I sighed and turned back to Ortega.

"Senator, what is it exactly you want me to do? Frankly, I think what you have here is a bunch of kids who have been too long in the remote areas of Peru. They have probably been visiting local paq yachaq, experimenting with mind-altering substances and gone out of their minds. Edwin Cooper told his son you had both investigated the Philadelphia Experiment together. When Danny died, one of his pals, suffering paranoia from too much ayahuasca, wrote to you as Carl Allen. It sucks, but that is not the kind of stuff we deal with, Senator. We deal with people who commit crimes against humanity. That's our remit."

He nodded, then he looked at his desktop and nodded some more.

"I know that, Harry. I can't tell you how or why, but I can tell you for certain that Carl Allen, in this letter, is warning me that there is a crime being committed against humanity even as we speak, down in the San Julian Valley. More than that, if we do not act soon, an even greater crime is going to be committed."

I sighed again, a little louder. "That the Supay, the spirits of the underworld, are going to rise up from Ukupacha, the underworld, and eat everybody's soul? You don't need me, Senator. You need Fox Mulder from the FBI."

"Don't get smart with me, Harry. You have to take it as read that I know what I am talking about. And the brigadier here will vouch for that."

I turned to look at the brigadier. He was watching me impassively. After a moment he nodded.

"I have known the senator for many years, Harry. He has been a client on many occasions, and I have never known him to be wrong. He has his sources, and I know them to be very reliable."

I scowled. "So what's the job? Track down the god of the underworld and kill him?"

The senator stared at me a moment. He looked mad. Then suddenly he laughed. He turned and laughed at the brigadier, pointing at me.

"Insolent focking son of a bitch. Ha! Ha! Ha!"

He stopped laughing as suddenly as he had started and said, "Yeah, pretty much that is what I want. Find Carl Allen, find out who he is and what he is talking about. Find out what he means by 'eating souls,' find out who's doing it and kill them."

"Do I get a choice in this?"

He cleared his throat and started fitting the letter and the envelope back in the plastic sleeve. I looked at the brigadier. He shook his head.

"OK, so when do I leave?"

The senator reached in another drawer and pulled out a large white envelope, which he dropped in front of me.

"Courtesy of the Central Intelligence Agency. Everything you need is in there. Go do what you do best, Harry. Buddy here will keep me posted."

I took the envelope and inspected the contents: a passport, a driver's permit and a credit card in the name of Henry Baumb—cute—a first-class ticket to Cusco and a slim manila file.

I stood. The brigadier and the senator exchanged handshakes, good wishes and a few shoulder-slaps, and we left the office in silence.

We walked down the echoing, marble corridor as far as the great, vaulted rotunda and stepped out into the bright sunshine, opposite the Capitol. There I stopped and the brigadier turned to face me. I spoke before he did.

"I thought we had an understanding. I choose my jobs. You are not my boss, sir. I don't work for you and this is not the army. And this..." I held up the manila envelope. "This job is bullshit!"

"Harry—"

He said it quietly, but he had that kind of authority that made you shut up and listen even if he only whispered. So I shut up and listened.

"In the first place Senator Ortega has the kind of pull that could put our budget in jeopardy. So you'll understand that I don't want to upset him, unless I have to."

"If you had to, would you?"

He didn't hesitate. "Yes. I will not compromise our principles or the way we operate."

"Isn't that exactly what you have just done?"

"No. And if you'll listen for a moment I'll explain why."

"Go ahead."

He looked away at the traffic cruising down the broad expanse of Independence Avenue. For a long moment he didn't speak. When he did he locked eyes with me.

"In the second place, Harry, I have a strong feeling that there is a lot more to this case than meets the eye. If you don't want to do it you don't have to. I'll face the music. But I want my best man on this. I don't want a professional killer with ice in his veins. I want a blade, a trooper from the Regiment, who can assess the situation and act accordingly."

There was no mistaking the seriousness in his voice. I narrowed my eyes.

"You're serious. What do you think is going on down there? You don't believe all this Aztec god's revenge crap, do you?"

"No." He blinked a couple of times. "But something is going on, and I want to know what. I would consider it a personal favor if you go and check it out. I also think you'll find there are deeper depths and levels than you suspect."

"Seriously?"

"Ortega discussed this case with...people; people who know about Cobra. They all agreed they wanted you to take the case. There is a lot more to this than meets the eye, Harry. Look into it, find out what is going on, and if you judge an execution is in order, you have the authority to carry it out."

"Judge, jury and executioner?"

He held my eye. "Is it the first time in your career you've had to do that?"

I thought about it. "No." And then, "OK, I'll do it."

TWO

Colonel Jane Harris, Cobra's Head of Operations, lived in a large, Victorian house on Potomac Avenue, a stone's throw from the Army's Dalecarlia Water Treatment Plant and the Renaissance Sibley Hospital. It was an elegant, yellow-brick, two-story affair with an elaborate wrought-iron veranda on both floors, which gave it a kind of colonial feel. It had a well-kept lawn out front bordered by thuja trees and rosebushes, and abundant trees poking over the black slate, gabled roof.

I sat in my TVR, staring at the house and wondering what the hell I was doing there. It was tacitly understood that though she was Head of Operations, the brigadier briefed me, and she and I kept our distance. It was a wise arrangement, and yet.

I climbed out of the beast, slammed the door and followed the stone path to the yellow brick house. There I leaned on the bell for a few seconds, and waited, detecting noises inside.

She opened the door and frowned at me. She was in Levi's, Converse trainers and a blue and white checked shirt. She looked like a '50s ad for milk. I smiled at her frown.

"Is this a bad time?"

She blinked hard and frowned harder. "Uh, no... Harry, what are you doing here?"

I shrugged. "I'm flying out tomorrow. Apparently there is a good chance I will have my soul sucked out and eaten by the Supay. I'm still not clear if that's a 'him' or a 'them,' but either way, he or they are coming up from Ukupacha, and I may get my soul eaten. I thought maybe I'd better come and say goodbye."

She stood staring up at me a moment, then added a sigh to make me feel a little bit more uncomfortable. I said, "If this is a bad time, you have company or anything…"

"It's not a bad time, Harry, and I haven't got company. Even if I had, it wouldn't matter. But…" She raised her open hands, then let them drop. "You'd better come in."

She stood back and I stepped inside. "Sure know how to make a guy feel welcome." I added a smile to show there was no hard feeling. She didn't respond and I followed her into her living room, where she sat on an elegant sage sofa which was looking good for its age. I figured a century at least.

She got straight to the point. "Harry, you know what the situation is."

"Are you going to ask me to sit down, or do I have to take this standing up?"

"Don't be absurd."

She gestured with a limp hand and a sage chair that matched the sage sofa, and shifted her butt so she was looking at me when I sat.

"Harry, you know what this job entails. You know we can't allow personal feelings to intrude."

I did something that ended up being a hybrid of a snort and a smile.

"I don't want to marry you, Jane. I was in DC, I expected you to be at the briefing. I thought I'd look in and see how you are. You're the Head of Operations, but I have barely seen you since the Yushbaev affair.[1]"

---

1. See *Breath of Hell*

She looked away. "You keep harping back to that, as though I don't feel guilty enough."

"There is no reason for you to feel guilty. You did what any mother would have done. Jane, this doesn't have to be complicated. We just..."

"It is complicated, Harry! Whether it has to be or not. We operate in a very tenuous gray area in the law, we cannot be like other people. We cannot behave like other people, and we certainly can't..."

She stopped herself.

"Can't what?"

She let her gaze drop to the floor and spoke softly. "We can't behave like ordinary people. Let's just leave it at that."

I said, "We can't even be friends?" and kicked myself for sounding like some lame, Californian high school soap.

She tried to look at me, but her eyes wound up staring out the window.

"The brigadier and I have spoken."

"That sounds ominous."

"We've discussed it, and we both agree it is probably best if you and I keep our contact to a minimum."

I felt the hot twist of anger in my gut. "Don't you think I would have been a better person to discuss that with?"

Now she looked at me, and her eyes were bright and angry and sad all at the same time.

"No! That's precisely it, Harry! You don't get it. This is not about you or me, it's about Cobra! And the work we do. You, me, our feelings, they are irrelevant! That is the whole point. So no, I should definitely not discuss it with you. I should discuss it with the brigadier because with this behavior, what you are doing right now, we are putting Cobra at risk. Your being here now puts Cobra at risk."

"So I should leave?"

Again her eyes went to the carpet.

"Yes, you should."

"Fine." I stood. "I am sorry I came and caused you embarrassment." Her eyes closed in a wince of pain. Anger and hurt drove me on. "I assure you it won't happen again."

I left her house with the hot burn of humiliation in my belly and in my cheeks. I drove back to my hotel on Maryland Avenue, ordered a sirloin steak and a bottle of mineral water, and studied the file the senator had given me, while I ate lunch on my balcony, overlooking the circus.

The file wasn't much: pictures of Liz Calder, pretty, blonde, thirty-something, a face that had grown accustomed to looking worried and defensive; pictures of Danny Cooper, the beach boy American dream, surfer, quarterback with a brain, honorable, good listener, all the girls are in love with him. I wondered if that included Liz Calder, and whether it was relevant.

More pictures, a couple of Alfredo Quispe, the mayor of San Julian, friend to foreigners, especially those with dollars, local landowner and patron of archeologists.

There wasn't a lot besides that. I had been booked in at Angie's Hostal in the town square, which was rather unimaginatively called Plaza de San Julian. The booking form told me I not only got my own bathroom and WiFi, I also got hot water twenty-four hours a day.

My weapons, a Sig Sauer P226 TacOps and a Fairbairn and Sykes commando fighting knife, had been sent on ahead to the hostel with special diplomatic customs clearance. According to the file Liz Calder and some of her team were also staying at Angie's.

I finished my meal, packed my case and spent a couple of hours in the hotel gym, working with weights to enhance power and speed. When I had finished my routine and I was headed for the showers a guy in his late twenties, with an unfashionable moustache and a chest like a beer vat, smiled at me and rose from the bench where he was doing sit-ups. I'd noticed he'd done about five hundred. He was sweating, but he wasn't out of breath.

"Excuse me—"

I looked at him and waited. He said, "Are you Harry Bauer?"

"Yeah, why?"

"I apologize for intruding, my name is Frank Cooper. Folks call me Frankie. Look, um..."

Every alarm bell in my body was ringing. "You have my attention, Mr. Cooper. What's on your mind?"

"Yeah, I'm sorry." He ran his fingers through his hair. "It's a kind of delicate subject. Could we talk somewhere private?"

I mopped my face with my towel and sighed. "Probably not. How long is this going to take?"

He held up his hands like I was going to shoot him. "Five, ten minutes most. It's about my brother."

"Danny."

His eyes widened. "Yes, you know?"

"Meet me in the cocktail lounge at seven. You've got ten minutes."

"Thank you, Mr. Bauer. I am truly grateful."

I skipped the shower, went up to my room, showered there and changed for dinner. At six-fifty I was down in the cocktail lounge leaning up against the bar. The place was quiet, so Johnny, the New York barman, sidled over and jerked his chin at me.

"You're from New York, right?"

"Born and bred."

"So you know the New York alphabet."

He was wiping down the bar, watching me. I shook my head. "Can't say I do."

"C'mon," he said in mock exasperation, "fuckin' A, fuckin' B, fuckin' C." I laughed. "That's the New York alphabet, man. What'll it be?"

"The Macallan, straight up." As he set up the glass I asked him, "You want to make an easy C-note?"

"Who do I have to kill?"

"Nothing that complicated. A nervous kid with a moustache is going to join me in about five minutes. When he's done with his drink, don't wash his glass, just put it in a plastic bag for me."

His eyebrows crawled up his balding head. "That's it?"

I grinned without humor. "I want to know if he's the father of my daughter's baby."

"He says he's not?"

"Son of a bitch."

"Consider it done. I always charge in advance. Company policy."

I slipped him a hundred dollars which he pocketed and poured me a generous measure of Scotch. A couple of minutes later Frank Cooper came into the bar, like a hesitant chicken, looking left and right before every step. I hailed him, he looked relieved and joined me as I sat at a table in the corner.

"Thanks again for seeing me, Mr. Bauer. I realize you must be a busy man."

"What makes you say that?"

He looked startled, and as he fumbled for an answer I watched his pupils, his complexion and the skin on his neck. I didn't see anything unusual. He finished up on, "I just assume, a man of your um, uh, standing, would be... I mean, I didn't mean anything by it, I just..."

"Say what you mean, mean what you say, Mr. Cooper. Now, what about your brother?"

"Oh, uh, Danny?"

I narrowed my eyes and looked for changes in his breathing, trembling of the hands. There was nothing at all.

"That's what you said, Mr. Cooper. You said Danny was your brother. Are you nervous for some reason?"

"No, well, yeah, a bit."

The waitress came over and smiled a question at Cooper. He said, "Oh, um...Coke," he gave a nervous laugh, "No zeros, just normal..."

"Original."

"That's the one."

She went away and he looked at me across the table. Before he could say, "Oh, um..." again I said, "What's making you nervous, Mr. Cooper?"

He looked at his hands cupped in his lap. "I don't know if you know it, Mr. Bauer, but you're a pretty intimidating guy."

"I know it," I said without inflection. "So how about we start with you telling me how you know who I am?"

He thought about it for a moment and now I saw his neck color slightly.

"My dad was in Delta Force."

"So what?"

The waitress brought over his Coke and set it in front of him with another cute smile.

"He did a few training exercises with the SAS. He said he met you on one of the exercises."

I allowed my mind to flow backward, searching for a Cooper. There was a Frank Cooper, years back, almost at the beginning. I barely remembered him.

"What was his name?"

"Frank, like me."

"How the hell does your father know I'm in DC?"

"He saw you this morning, at Cannon House. He's head of security there."

I leaned forward. "First, how the hell did he see me and I didn't see him?"

"He saw you on camera and after a moment he recognized you."

"Second, why are you talking to me instead of him?"

"He was going to, but he thought it would attract too much attention, so he checked the visitors' log and saw where you were staying." I sat back in my seat. It was credible. He went on, "Dad said that if anybody could find out what happened to Danny, you could."

I shook my head. It was too much of a coincidence. "He must know a hundred guys as good as me."

"No." He shook his head with feeling. "He said the guys you

were with, Captain Walker, Sergeant Hays, Sergeant Gordon and you, were the best he'd ever seen."

I sipped my whisky and as I set the glass down I asked him, "So what's your brother done?"

"He's dead."

"There's not much I can do for him, then, is there?"

"But Dad, and me, we want to know what happened. He was down in Peru, on an archeological dig, he was enjoying himself." He gave a small laugh. "It was like a dream come true for him. He was crazy about archeology, especially the Incas and the Maya and all that. But one day he grabs one of the Jeeps, drives to the top of the mountain where the dig was, and just throws himself off. Why would he do that?"

I scowled at him. "I don't know. Why would I? What is it exactly you and your dad expect me to do?"

"Look," he swallowed hard, "my dad knows that you're going to Peru, to investigate the dig." He held up both hands like I might be about to hit him. "He doesn't know why! He doesn't know any details. But he knows you're going, and he's willing to pay, whatever price you name, if you'll find out what happened to Danny."

I narrowed my eyes and shook my head, thinking fast. "You must be out of your mind, both of you. I don't know what you're talking about."

I was about to stand, but he stopped me. "I have information that will be useful to you."

"What information?"

"Letters, letters Danny sent us just before he died. He said there was something weird going on. He didn't know what it was. It's best if you read them."

"Get the hell out of here. I'm going to have dinner. Come to my room at ten and bring the letters. I'll give you an answer then."

He nodded eagerly. "Thank you, Mr. Bauer. I am incredibly grateful. Thank you so much."

"Shut up. You're making a scene. Go."

I took my time over dinner, thinking things through from every angle. At nine-fifty I ordered a Macallan and told the waiter I'd be right back, I had forgotten something in my room. I was unlocking the door when Cooper appeared climbing the stairs. He approached me in silence. I pushed the door open and indicated he should go inside. I left the door open and followed him as far as the desk, where he reached into his inside pocket.

I put my left hand firmly on his right wrist, pressing it hard against his chest, and smashed a right hook hard into his floating ribs. As he doubled up, wheezing, I reached inside his jacket, for whatever it was he was reaching for.

As I had expected, there were no letters. There was a long, razor-sharp stiletto in a slim holster under his arm. I grabbed him by the scruff of his neck and the seat of his pants, rushed him to the balcony and heaved him over. He didn't scream, he was winded, but he did make a sickening thud.

"Do your homework, schmuck," I told him, too late for it to be of any use. "Danny's father was Edwin, not Frank."

I went down to the dining room and finished my Scotch, wondering what it meant.

THREE

I HAD THE GLASS JOHNNY HAD BAGGED FOR ME SENT BY special messenger to Cobra for DNA analysis. They worked on it overnight and in the morning, as I was waiting to board the plane, the lab called me and told me they'd got no hits on CODIS, but they had Danny Cooper's body, pending investigation, and they had compared his DNA with the DNA on the glass. The two were not related. The guy I'd thrown over the balcony was not Danny Cooper's brother. That much I knew.

I called the brigadier.

"It was a hit," he'd said. "Somebody has put a contract out on you."

First-class passengers were boarding and I stood to join the line.

"I'd got that far, sir. The problem is, whoever put out that contract knows about this job, in some detail, but not enough to know the Senator had told us about Danny's father. That must narrow the field a bit."

"Yes, it does. But he didn't offer the information, Harry. You forced his hand. The contract may already have been granted by then, and the agent already formulated his plan of approach, assuming you had no idea who Danny was." He sighed. "All right,

I'll take care of it at this end. But be alert, they may well send somebody after you to Peru."

"Yeah, but the question is who? Who might?"

I T   W A S   A   L O N G, tedious seventeen hours via Miami and Lima, where there was a delay to the connecting flight, so that I finally got through passport control in Cusco at eight AM, almost eighteen hours after departing DC. Odin had arranged for a Land Rover Defender V8 to be waiting for me at the airport. The airport had been modern in the '70s. Now the marble was dusty and the cracks were showing, and it was small enough for me to find the information desk, where I picked up the keys. The truck was outside the door, in the parking lot. I slung my bags in the trunk and, having slept for over twelve hours on the plane, I was ready for some breakfast.

Cusco International Airport is actually inside the city. So I stopped at one of the small, seedy cafés outside the main gate, on Avenida Velasco Astete. The waiter wanted to give me a bowl of chicken soup, but I managed to persuade him to give me a gallon of strong, black coffee instead, with buttered toast. He smiled and shrugged and went to get my order.

By the time I was finished it was nine AM. The sun was shining and the forecast was for a maximum of sixty-nine degrees. I climbed in the Land Rover and set off west down the shabby, dusty road. I decided I liked Peru—or at least I liked Cusco. It seemed to have an uncomplicated, comfortable shabbiness to it. It was noisy and bustling, but when you looked at people's faces, they didn't look like they were on the edge of a coronary. They were cool. This was definitely not New York, or DC.

I headed down the Avenue 28th July, wondering why Spanish-speaking countries always give their avenues dates. At the Pachacutec Oval I took the Avenida del Ejercito—literally the Avenue of the Army, you gotta love Latin America—and pretty soon I was winding my way up into the hills along a road that may once have been asphalt. I drove past shabby, concrete buildings, perched on uneven, irregular sidewalks, that all looked like nineteenth-century warehouses, or prisons. They were all painted every ugly color you could think of.

Here was one painted army green at the bottom, and dirty white up top. It had a sign by a large wooden door advertising cold beer and Coke. The one next to it was peeling royal blue at the bottom and the same dirty white from halfway up the wall to the corrugated roof. The one after that, on the opposite side of the road, was oxblood red all over. That one had a terrace with tables and chairs, and two sleeping dogs. Interspersed with these solid, ugly buildings were a multitude of oddly-shaped houses, mostly bare concrete and brick, like there had been a building boom and suddenly all the money had dried up.

Another twenty minutes and I was out of the scrappy suburbs and climbing into dense mountain woodlands, headed toward Chaqquerec and Maras. Pretty soon it became remote and desolate, with only sporadic buildings seen fleetingly through the undergrowth.

The going was slow and it took me an hour of winding and weaving to reach Urubumba, where I was able to cross the Urubumba River.

After that, the bizarre, otherworldly landscapes of the Andes enfolded me. Towering green conical mountains rising suddenly among the rainforest, the deep chasms between them, and the clouds trapped among them, all added to a growing sense of remoteness and isolation. This was the Sacred Valley of the Incas, and you could see why.

I drove through the bizarre valley of Ollantaytambo, situated at the junction of three massive canyons, and glimpsed from afar the ancient Inca fortress. From what I had read on the plane, some of the rocks used to build the place weighed fifty tons and more, and fit so snuggly together you couldn't fit a razorblade between them.

Progress became slower the higher I climbed into the Andes.

The road made one hairpin bend after another climbing the faces of the mountains, so that after driving several miles you had only really advanced a mile, or a little more. But once I had passed Umasbamba, the road straightened out and I began to descend toward Santa Maria, a small town on the banks of the Urumbamba. I thought about stopping for lunch, but I was getting tired of wending and weaving through mountains and jungles, and pressed on for another ten miles or so, following the river upstream, until I came to Quillabamba.

There I crossed the cute, quiet, clean town, crossed the Urubamba, and began to climb again, not through jungle now, but through wild, rolling escarpments up into the foothills of Apusupay, the mountain of the spirits from the Underworld.

Finally, having covered just seventy miles as the crow flies, in six hours, I entered the tiny town of San Julian.

It was much like other Andean towns. There was a central square, though in San Julian it was more of a cobbled circus, dominated by a large, sandstone church. A great, arched door stood at the front, closed, and two towers rose at each side above the façade, each with its own iron bell, to call the faithful to their knees. All around the church ancient houses swarmed, some whitewashed, others painted garish colors: blue, orange, yellow, even brown. All of them with corrugated tile roofs.

At the center of the circus was a garden with a fountain, benches, arbors and rosebushes, so that for a moment you could imagine you were at some Mediterranean holiday resort, until you saw the eerie backdrop of the overpowering, soaring Andes.

To the left of the Church of San Julian was a block of colonial buildings, painted blue and yellow and pink. They had inviting terraces out front, with tables and chairs, vines and palms, and plenty of convenient parking space.

The yellow building, which looked as though it might have been flown over from Paris in the Belle Époque, had a hand-painted sign over the big door which read, Angie's Hostal. There were orange trees on half-barrels and also cream, calico parasols that didn't advertise Coke. What I could see of the inside had a lot of dark wood and polished brass.

I swung down from the cab, grabbed my bags from the trunk and went inside. It was practically empty but for a blonde woman in her thirties wearing a Harvard sweatshirt with the sleeves pushed up to her elbows. She was washing glasses in very soapy water, and kept trying to blow a strand of hair out of her left eye.

I dropped my bags on the floor and leaned on the bar. I smiled and she watched me around her lock of hair.

"You Angie?"

"I hope not." She was Australian, or at least Antipodian. "Angie died in 1903."

I nodded. "Well, if you are, you're looking pretty good for a woman who's been dead for a hundred and eighteen years."

She picked up a hand towel and dried her hands.

"That might be a compliment, then again, it might not. Name's Cas. What can I get you?"

"Right now, a lot of things, Cas. I have a room booked in the name of Harry Baumb, with a view of the square if that is possible."

She had a laptop behind the bar. She rattled at it and said, "Yup. Indefinite stay, room one-A. It's actually a suite, with a little lounge, bedroom, balcony and bathroom."

"With hot water twenty-four hours a day." She laughed. I said, "I am also going to need a large steak and fries, and several extremely cold beers."

"You just drove from Cusco, right?" She reached under the counter and pulled out a heavy package addressed to me. She put it on the counter. "It doesn't rattle and it doesn't tick."

I treated her to my best lopsided smile. "But it does go boom."

She gave a throaty laugh that was somehow alluring. "No bell-boy, no lift—that's an elevator to you—up the stairs, first door on your right. I'll give you twenty minutes for a shower and start making your grub. How's that?"

"That sounds just about perfect."

The room was large and airy, with high ceilings and two sets of tall, French doors with green slatted shutters, that gave onto a balcony overlooking the square. There was a threadbare blue sofa and a couple of chairs I figured the original Angie had brought with her from Australia. There was also an odd assortment of mahogany antiques with inlaid flowers and swirls, and a bare floor of large, terracotta tiles.

The bedroom was of similar proportions, only it had a large, brass bed in the center of the room, with a huge puffy quilt and enormous pillows.

I hung my clothes in the freestanding mahogany wardrobe and stepped into the shower. The plumbing gave a Jurassic groan when I turned on the taps, but the water came out hot, as promised.

When I had dried off and dressed, I opened the package from the brigadier and found a Sig Sauer P226 TacOps, four magazines and a Fairbairn and Sykes commando knife. I put the lot in the drawer in my bedside table and went down for cold beer and rare steak.

Outside the shadows were already growing long. Night falls very suddenly at the equator, at around six o'clock, and up in the mountains it was that much more sudden due to the high peaks.

There was no dining room as such. Instead, she had sectioned off a part of the bar, where she had seven or eight heavy, wooden tables set with napkins, cutlery and a candle. There was no one sitting there when I came down. Lunch was over and dinner was a couple of hours off yet.

Leaning on the bar there was a tall, blond kid in khaki Bermudas, heavy boots and thick woolen socks. The boots were scuffed and dusty, and he had dirt on his knees. I went and leaned on the bar beside him. Cas was pulling him a beer. She waved her eyebrows at me and glanced at a clock on the wall as she handed the kid his beer.

"Your timing always this good?"

"When I get the right kind of cooperation, sure."

She gave her appealing chortle. "You're going to be trouble, I can tell."

"You want to give me one of those?" I turned to the guy in the khaki shorts. He had drained the beer and was wiping his mouth. "I guess you needed that. You been digging?"

"Yup. On both counts!" He laughed. I held out my hand. "Harry."

He offered me his elbow, then laughed and shook. "Earl. Can't get my head around all the elbows and face masks. Doesn't seem real, especially up here." I gestured at Cas to give Earl another. He pointed at me, with his blond eyebrows raised high above his pale blue eyes. "You have a disease which makes it hard to breathe? Hey, you know what, we'll have you breathing your own carbon dioxide all day, maybe that'll cure it, right? In the beginning only the old and the infirm died from it, remember? After a year of face masks, everyone is going down."

I smiled. "Politicians," I said, "they don't see a problem, they see an opportunity."

He held up his glass and toasted. "Cheers!"

"So, you're an archeologist?"

"Postgrad. I was lucky to get on this dig. It's going to be pretty amazing."

"Why's that?"

He raised both hands, like he was holding a ball, and drew breath, then looked sidelong at Cas. "You sure you're interested? Cas tells me I am a pain in the ass when I get started."

"You're OK. Cas can go and get me a steak. I'm interested."

Cas went away and Earl got started.

"OK, this is the Sacred Valley of the Incas, right? And traditional archeology attributes all the cities, fortresses, towns, etcetera in this region to the Incas. But there has always been a problem."

"What's that?"

"The...," he screwed up his face, "enormous stones they used. I mean you are talking about fifty, sixty, even a hundred tons of solid granite. And then, these stones were cut so precisely that you could barely fit a razorblade between one stone and another." He shook his head. "And we are not talking about the interlocking grid construction of bricks. No, sir, they knew how to do that, that's clear from the Coricancha temple which rivals anything we could do today, but no, instead, we are talking about each stone being a different shape and size, and weight, and being cut to fit exactly. I mean, the question was always, how in the hell did they do that?"

"Cut it..."

"Cut it, sometimes several miles down one mountain and up another, and having got it from the quarry to the building site, raise it forty, fifty feet in the air and place it, with fractional precision, into its corresponding place."

"So how did they do it?"

His eyes went wide with wonder. "Nobody knows! Nobody knows. But the mystery deepens, Harry, because..."

Cas came out of the kitchen with my steak.

"I warned you. You gonna eat at the bar?"

"I'll sit at the table." I jerked my head at Earl. "You want to join me while you finish your beer?"

"Sure." We moved to the table and he kept talking as he sat. "See, here's the thing. If the techniques they used were something simple, like rollers or wet sand, like some people suggest, aside from the impracticality of it, that is not the kind of technique you forget, right? We've been building houses with pretty much the same techniques for the past ten thousand years, we haven't forgotten. So, how come, if the Incas were using basic logs and wet sand, how come they forgot how to do it, and suddenly, started building with small rocks piled on top of each other any old how, like a basic drystone wall?"

I cut into my steak and shook my head. "I don't know. Is that what happened?"

He sighed. "That's the thing. Nobody knows what happened, but the techniques they used for those megalithic buildings were forgotten. The problem is, it is really hard to date stone, so it is impossible to date the buildings. We can infer from circumstantial evidence when the buildings were probably made."

He took a pull on his beer and wiped his mouth.

"It also complicates things that Inca architecture varies according to whether it is coastal or interior, but the fact remains, nobody remembers how to make these megalithic structures, and when the Spanish conquistadores arrived, they had already forgotten. And remember...," he wagged a finger at me, "they chose to build this way. They could have made equally magnificent structures with much easier techniques, smaller, more manageable stones, but they chose to do it this way. It's like us making factories out of massive sheets of molded steel instead of using bricks. On the face of it, that's real hard, but when you know how, it's easy."

I was halfway through my steak and paused to pull off half my beer.

"So what you're saying is that they had some technique which made it easier to use huge stones, but that technique has been lost."

He pointed at me. "Exactly. A twelve-year-old kid could lay bricks in an intersecting grid. He might need to practice, but he understands the basic principle established back in the mists of time. We all do. That's a skill our culture will never forget. But ask him, or me or you, to make a steel prefab. That is a skill that could disappear in a single generation."

I gave him a lopsided grin. "You're not going to tell me aliens built them."

"Nah." He shrugged. "I'm not going to tell you they didn't, either. I am open to the possibility, but one thing I am going to tell you is that they had techniques that we have not got today. There is not a construction company in the world today that can carry a one-hundred-ton slab of granite three or four miles up a mountainside."

I finished the steak and wiped my mouth, and signaled Cas for two more beers.

"And you think that in your dig you have found the answer to what that technique was?"

Outside, dusk was closing in and amber lights were coming on. Laughter and the scraping of chairs said people were gathering on the terrace. A couple of waiters had joined Cas and I had the feeling the evening was getting underway. I saw Earl eyeing the door. He shrugged, suddenly apparently uninterested. "Who knows, we'll have to wait and see."

I glanced at the door and saw a woman I recognized. She had her hair pulled back into a severe ponytail, a khaki shirt knotted at her waist and denim shorts she'd made out of a pair of Levi's. On her feet she had big walking boots and heavy socks rolled down to the ankle. She was standing looking at Earl.

"Earl, we're all outside. You going to join us?"

His cheeks flushed. "Oh, hi, Liz. I was just talking to Harry here—"

"Yeah, I can see that." She looked at me long enough for me to smile and say, "Hi, Liz," and for her to ignore me and turn back to Earl. "On your way you can bring some beers with you. Make it six cold ones."

Earl half got to his feet and looked apologetic. "I'm sorry. She's an amazing archeologist and an extraordinary person, but..." He shrugged.

I supplied the rest. "She's special. Don't sweat it. Go secure your career."

"Thanks. I'll see you around."

"You will."

FOUR

I ordered a Scotch and an espresso and spent an hour reading about the Incas, and clarifying in my mind how they were different from the Aztecs and the Maya. I had got as far as the fact that they were centered in Peru, had managed to build a sprawling empire that lasted three hundred years and spanned hundreds of towns, cities and fortresses—all connected by a network of roads—all without ever developing iron, wheels or a writing system, when Cas sidled over and sat down. I closed the book and set it on the table.

"Don't let me interrupt you."

"Why not?"

She closed her eyes and shook her head. "You can be such an arsehole." She grinned. "Forgive me, but I feel like I can say that to you even though we've only just met."

"I used to live in England. I know what an arsehole is. The least you can do now is have a drink with me."

She signaled the waiter to bring over a bottle and a glass.

"It eases off around now." She said it like she was justifying it to herself. Then she pointed at the book. "So what brings you to Peru? You an Inca nerd?"

"Nope. But I am intrigued. As far as I am aware there are three things you need to make an empire: Iron weapons with which to subdue the people you conquer, wheels with which to carry those weapons out to the countries you are conquering, and writing so you can write laws for your subjects, and keep accounts of who is paying you how much."

She shrugged. "That's why this place attracts so many UFO and conspiracy freaks. So if it's not the Incas, what is it?"

I eyed her a moment, wondering what to tell her. The waiter came over and put a bottle of Black Label and a glass on the table. She poured. I said:

"Two things. The secondary reason is that I am looking for somewhere to invest my money. I don't want the IRS to get their dirty little hands on it, and I would like to invest it in something interesting and worthwhile."

She was frowning. "Like what? A cute little Andean hotel?"

"I was thinking more like research into green medicine, ancient cultures..."

"Huh, you'll get both of those here. And the other reason?"

"I'm looking for a friend who came out here some time back. Last I heard of him he was in Peru studying the Incas. Then I didn't hear from him anymore. His phone went dead and he disappeared. I wrote a couple of times, but got no response. I figured he might be around here drinking himself into an early grave."

"Oooh," she said, "there is a squidgy center under that hard exterior."

"Squidgy? Is that a thing in Australia?"

"It's a thing in New Zealand. We have a lot of people drinking themselves into an early grave here, what's your pal's name?"

"Carl, Carl Allen."

She frowned. "Nothing comes to mind. What does he look like?"

I realized I didn't know and tried to be artfully vague. "Kind of average, hard to describe. Last time he wrote to me he was talking a lot about the Supay, evil spirits that were coming up from Ukupacha, like hell or the underworld."

"I'll ask around, maybe somebody will know something. A photograph would help."

"Yeah, I'll give you one when I unpack." I sipped and smacked my lips. "So what gives with the iron maiden outside?"

"Oh, Liz, her bark is worse than her bite. She runs the dig up the hill on Apusupay. She runs a pretty tight ship and she likes to keep things under control. I don't know if it's true or if she's bullshitting, but rumor has it she's made some pretty important finds."

"Huh, any chance you could introduce me?"

Her cheeks colored and she forced a smile. "Why, do you fancy her?"

I smiled and shook my head. "No, I just think she might know where Carl is, or one of her worker ants might."

"Oh, OK, next time she goes to the bar, but I warn you, she does not welcome intrusion."

"Yeah, I kind of got that. So who else is in town who's interesting?"

She arched an eyebrow. "You looking for somebody in particular?"

"Yeah, I told you, my pal Carl. Aside from him, not really." I shrugged and made like I was thinking. "Except maybe somebody interesting who is doing something worthwhile I could invest in."

She raised her shoulders.

"Well, there's the other woman in town."

I laughed out loud. "The other woman? Who's the guy?"

"Get your mind out of the gutter, Harry. We just happen to have two strong women in town at the moment. Dr. Amanda Epstein. She's one of those intense, driven women who believe in saving all the children."

"Don't you?"

"Of course, but who doesn't, right? So I don't go making a big song and dance about it so everybody can look at me and say how amazing I am."

"You don't like her, huh?"

"Gosh, you must be really sensitive and intuitive. Nah..." She shrugged and flapped a hand at me. "She's OK, she just overdoes the future Nobel Prize act. She's doing research down in La Boca del Diablo. Now there's somewhere you could invest your money."

"The Devil's Mouth? What is that, a nightclub?"

"No, just to the east of here there is a deep ravine, what you Yanks would call a canyon."

"We call them ravines, too."

"It runs for almost ten miles from the top of Apusupay all the way down to the Urubamba River, and it is really, really dense jungle. I don't know if you are aware of this, but the Peruvian Andes have the richest biodiversity on the planet, more even than the Brazilian Amazon."

"I didn't know that, no."

"So anyway, about halfway up the ravine, or canyon, there is a huge rocky outcrop, like a huge overhang, and at the bottom it kind of plunges down into a huge depression. And I do mean huge, about half a mile across, and there are apparently caves, plants and insects in there which are unique. And she, all credit where credit is due, is working in that hellhole with her team, looking for fuck-knows what—a cure for cancer, Alzheimer's, erectile dysfunction..." She shrugged and shook her head. "Whatever it is, she's been there almost a year, and whenever I see her she's smiling, she looks fresh as a daisy, all smiles, beautiful skin. God, I hate her."

I laughed. "But she's not staying here at your hotel?"

"See? You already want to meet her. No, she 's staying at the Pachacutec Inca Yupanqui hotel, a stone's throw from here. And no, I won't give you a refund if you switch hotels."

"I wouldn't dream of it. I had a sergeant in the army who was a New Zealander, and hearing you talk is pleasantly nostalgic. It reminds me of him."

She smiled. "I remind you of a sergeant in the army. You son of a bitch."

"That's what my mother used to call me."

I poured her another shot of Scotch. She didn't protest but said, "You know I still have to run this place and close up, right?"

"One for the road. You live in the hotel, right?"

"Don't get any funny ideas, mister."

"All my ideas are funny. I wanted to ask you, did you ever meet Danny?"

The smile faded from her face like she'd sprung a leak. She looked down at the table for a long moment, touched her drink with a finger, as though she was going to push it away, then picked it up and knocked it back.

"I guess you did."

"Yeah, I knew Danny." She frowned at me. "Who are you? You're flirting away, but all the while you're probing and asking questions. You a cop or something?"

I shook my head. "Carl mentioned Danny in his last letter."

She became serious. "What did he say about him?"

I held her eye, wondering how far I could push. I decided to risk it.

"He said he thought there was something odd about his death. He was a graduate from Arizona, right?" She nodded. "He became depressed and one day climbed to the top of the Apusupay and threw himself off."

"That's about the size of it. It happened about six months ago."

"You were close?"

"I was fond of him. We used to talk. He was fun." She shrugged one shoulder and looked away. "I guess we got pretty close."

I leaned forward, folded my arms on the table and frowned at her.

"Cas, is something going on here?"

She glanced outside, then looked me in the face. "I don't know what you mean. I don't know what you're talking about."

She should have got up and walked away on that, but she didn't. She sat there, staring into my face. I nodded and sank back in my chair. As I did so, as though responding to my own movement, she leaned forward and half whispered, "You show up out of the blue, in a thousand-dollar suit, driving a hundred-thousand-dollar Land Rover V8, asking questions about Danny and Carl Allen, and Liz and Amanda Epstein... Who are you? Share and share alike, Harry." She wagged a finger at me in the negative. "You don't get to play me."

I gave a single nod. "Understood."

"So what are you doing here?"

I held her eye a moment, then spoke carefully and slowly.

"I am here to find out what happened to Danny. Danny had friends in high places."

Her eyebrows shot up. "Danny?"

I smiled. "You'd be surprised. I came here straight from DC. I need to find out what happened to Danny, and Carl."

"You're not a cop?"

"I'm not a cop. American cops have no jurisdiction in Peru, Cas."

"I know that, Harry. I mean, you're not CIA or anything like that?"

"I am not CIA or anything remotely similar," I said, truthfully.

"So you're a private investigator."

"Yes, and that is all I can tell you, Cas. Believe me, you don't want to know any more. I don't want anyone to get hurt. I just want to know what's going on here, why he became depressed..."

I was not prepared for the strength of her reaction. Suddenly her eyes were burning and she snapped: "He was not depressed!"

"He wasn't?"

"No." She became sullen. I waited but she didn't say anything. After a moment I said, "Maybe you should tell me exactly what happened between you and Danny."

"Maybe I should, but not now. I have to close up soon, and I'm getting drunk, thanks to you." She looked me in the eye. "Another one of your techniques?" She gave a single, dry laugh. "And there was me thinking we'd hit it off."

"We had."

"Sure."

"Cas, I'm sorry. But I need to know. More to the point, his family needs to know."

"And his friends in high places."

"No." I shook my head. "They don't need to know. They're just helping out his family." She sighed. I added, "Besides, come to think of it, you are probably the highest-placed friend he has."

She looked up at me, but there wasn't much humor in her face. "Up in the Andes. That's funny," she said, but she didn't mean it.

"Cas, I work in a dirty profession, but I don't do dirty jobs. I am trying to help some people who lost their son—and Carl," I added, "who has no family. I'm not a saint, but I do what I can to redress the balance sometimes, in a world where too often the bad guys take the prize and the Dannies and Carls fall down steep canyons." I shrugged one shoulder and spread one hand. "Trouble is, sometimes, when I am digging around in all the bullshit, nice people like you get splashed. I'm sorry. I mean it."

She was quiet for a while, then said, "You mean you can't just walk up to your prime suspect and ask, 'Excuse me, could you please tell me what happened to Danny Cooper?'"

I smiled. "Most of the time that doesn't work. I wouldn't suggest you become a private eye. Best you stick to running a really cute hotel. That you do really well."

She sighed. "You almost sound sincere. OK, Harry. I need to

get back to my cute hotel. The whisky is on the house. We'll talk later."

I sat a while, nursing a nightcap and drumming my fingers on my book and wondering at a people who could build an empire that covered half a continent, without using wheels, iron or writing; who could build cities and fortresses with fifty-ton, precision-cut stones, without wheels, iron or writing. Did Danny's death have something to do with them? Or did it have a much more prosaic explanation? Most times men died because of money, power or women. And women died because of money, power and men. Most people don't die because of the Incas.

I was about to down my last shot for the night and hit the sack when a figure loomed in the door and came to lean with her hands on the back of the chair to my left. She had a severe pony-tail, a khaki shirt knotted at her waist and un-hemmed, cut-off Levi's. I couldn't see them, but I could sense the presence of her big walking boots.

I smiled. "Dr. Calder."

She didn't smile back. "You're asking questions about Danny."

"That's true. Would you like to sit down?"

"No. But I suppose I'd better." She turned and yelled in the general direction of the bar. "Cas! Gimme a shot glass here!" She pulled out the chair and sat. "Are you going to be a pain in my ass? I have a lot of work and a lot to do, and I am running out of funding and time. I do not need to get caught up in a lot of extraneous shit."

"Is that what Danny's death is, extraneous shit?"

She didn't flinch. "Yes."

"I think his family might disagree."

"And they'd be right. For them his life and death are deeply important. To me they are extraneous shit. Importance, Mr. Baum, is subjective. It's all about how a given thing affects me or you. There is no universal, objective standard for whether a thing is important or not. So don't even dream about trying to guilt trip me into caring about Danny's death. You'll be wasting both your time and mine."

I smiled to myself. Real honesty is so rare that when we encounter it head-on, it is hard to know how to deal with it.

"OK, so what to I need to do to get your help?"

"I'm here, offering it to you now. The deal is this: get it over and done with, then get out of my hair."

FIVE

A KID OF ABOUT FOURTEEN WITH THE SHADOW OF A moustache on his lip brought a shot glass for Dr. Calder. She filled her glass and pushed the bottle toward me. I watched her take a sip, smack her lips and sigh, then said: "It might not be that easy."

She groaned and rolled her eyes. "I knew you were going to say that."

She poured herself another shot. I asked her, "Do you know what happened to Danny?"

She threw back the drink and smacked her lips again. "Yes."

"What?"

"Hormones happened to Danny Cooper. Hormones! You should know all about that. Men are always telling women that the explanation for their absurd behavior is hormones. So here is the explanation for Danny Cooper's absurd behavior: hormones."

"You want to explain that for me, Dr. Calder?"

"Danny was twenty-four going on fourteen. He was very excited about having been selected for the dig. Too excited for a man his age. And while he was here he met two women: Dr. Amanda Epstein, whom any man—or woman for that matter—would have to be blind, deaf and mentally retarded not to fall in love with, I might well be in love with her myself if I paid any attention to her; and Cas, who I should imagine is also very easy to fall in love with. So Danny, being a total schmuck, fell in love with both of them."

I reached for my drink. "He fell in love with Dr. Epstein?"

"I just told you he did. I am not going to waste time confirming what I just told you. Give me some more of this."

I poured her another shot. "So, we humans are so astonishingly badly designed in every conceivable way, that if a man becomes infatuated with two women at the same time, instead of enjoying the one who accepts him, he will become obsessed with the one who turns him down. And that is what Danny did. Cas was really very taken with him, and took him to her crib more than once."

She knocked back her third shot and wiped her mouth.

"I'm willing to bet Cas is a damn good lay," she went on, "probably better than Epstein, but that fool Danny couldn't stop mooning over the one that got away, who had always been well out of his league. In the end he became so depressed he took one of my Jeeps to the top of the Apusupay, and, staring into the yawning void of his own existence, decided it wasn't worth the candle and jumped."

We sat staring at each other for a moment. Then I asked her, "Do you do it for effect, or are you actually like this?"

"Both." After a moment she allowed herself a small smile, and suddenly her humanity was there. "He might have fallen for me too. I'm pretty good-looking, but my personality puts men off."

I returned the ghost of her smile with a ghost of my own. "That's a conversation for another day and another bottle of Scotch. Do you know Carl?"

"Carl who?"

"That's a good question. He may not be Carl at all. He signed himself Carl Allen in a letter he sent me. He wrote in caps and in various different inks, green, red, blue. He might be Carlos Allende. He might be John Smith. He was concerned that the

Supay would be coming out of the tunnels from Ukupacha, and they were going to eat everybody's souls. According to Carl Allen, or whatever his name is, Danny knew about this and tried to stop it. That's why he died."

She listened very carefully, turning her glass in her fingers. When I'd finished she studied my face a moment.

"And you believe this?"

"I don't believe anything, Dr. Calder. I have a suspicion Danny may have discovered something he wasn't supposed to discover, tried to inform either the Peruvian or the American authorities, and got pushed into the yawning void of his own existence for his troubles."

She leaned forward slightly. "You think I killed him?"

"Did you?"

"Of course not."

"Why 'of course'? What makes it obvious you didn't kill him?"

"Well, for a start I just got through telling you the last damn thing I want is more problems. I cannot afford to get personally involved with my crews. And you need to be pretty involved with someone to throw them off a mountain."

"That's called piggy-backing."

"What?"

"You make two statements. The second one is obviously true, and the first one, which is less obvious, is accepted as obvious by the listener because it is riding 'piggy-back' on the first. It is obviously true that you need to be very involved with someone to throw them off a mountain. It is not so obviously true that you can't afford to get personally involved with your crew." I shrugged. "It might be true, but it's not obviously so."

"Again, subjective objective. It may not be obvious to you, but it is to me. And if you ask my crew..."

I cut in, "And may I ask your crew?" She sighed. "Or do I just have to take your word for all this?"

She sagged back in her chair. "Come to the dig, talk to the

crew, get it over and done with. Then please, leave us alone so we can do our job."

"I'll do that. What time are you there?"

"From just before first light. The crew turn up around seven thirty or eight."

"Good. Thank you, Dr. Calder."

"Call me Liz." The look of surprise on my face prompted her to explain. "There are four syllables in Dr. Calder. There is one in Liz. These small things accumulate by the end of a day."

She showed me that ghost of a smile again, stood and went to join her people outside.

I took a bottle of water upstairs, had another shower and went to bed.

The next morning, when I went down for breakfast at seven, Cas was not there but the Peruvian waitress told me Dr. Liz Calder had left at six to go to the dig. I had a couple of strong black coffees, got directions from the waitress and headed out of town on the Chancomayo Road and then turned right for the archeological dig, about a mile up the dirt track that climbed the western face of the Apusupay Mountain.

The sun was rising over the densely forested peaks to the east, where a lingering, golden mist rested on the canopy of trees. I took it easy, with the windows open, feeling the fresh morning air and listening to the wild variety of birdsong: echoing whoops, clicks and cries, and I was suddenly intensely aware that this impenetrably dense forest that smothered the mountains as far as the eye could see, was the very same one that swept down, out of the Andes and across Brazil and Colombia, as far as Surinam and French Guiana on the Atlantic coast of the continent, two thousand miles away. The feeling was at once liberating and claustrophobic. It brought home forcefully just how remote this place was.

After five or ten minutes rattling and bouncing up the track, I came to a fork. To the right the track continued, broad and potholed, up toward the distant peak of Apusupay, among patches of dense forest and green pasture. To the left, the track wound down the slope, around a large outcrop of rocks and earth. I turned here and followed the path among green meadows dotted with yellow and white flowers, to the large outcrop, where it turned right again.

Now I was looking down into the deep gorge that cloved the land between Apusupay and the next mountain. The bottom of the ravine, far below, was densely forested and I knew that a few miles down the line Amanda Epstein had her own research going on.

A little closer, three or four hundred yards away, where the mountainside bulged and curved around, I could see the suggestion of ancient terracing, above that, where the track led. There were a couple of trucks and people moving about. I headed that way, weaving around the rocks and the holes that peppered the road. The dig itself remained invisible until I had parked alongside a couple of battered Toyotas and a Jeep on a small esplanade, and swung down from the cab. Ahead of me the ground was relatively flat, beaten repeatedly by feet and the wheels of heavy vehicles, but over on the right, just where the steep wall of Apusupay began to climb again, I saw the broad head of a path marked out by wooden stakes. When I got there I found the path was made of a series of broad, shallow steps. Where they led made me stop and stare.

Against the deep, rich green of the mountains, the dig was a splatter of yellow and ocher sand, and rising from it, like Picasso's vision of a herd of elephants, were vast gunmetal walls made of stones that were each the size of a small house. Each was irregular in shape, each contained sharp angles that fit snuggly into the adjoining rocks. The wall I was looking at was easily forty to fifty feet in height.

The path followed the contour of the wall, passed a huge doorway with a lintel that was bigger than my Land Rover, and eventually wound down to a broad expanse of flat land where sections had been cordoned off and a lot of young people in denim shorts and straw hats were hunkered down scraping through the dirt. Among them I identified Liz Calder, and as though by some kind of intuition, she turned and squinted at me, blocking out the morning sun with her hand on her brow. She raised her hand in an unenthusiastic wave and started picking her way across the dig toward me. I started down the steps toward her.

We met at the vast doorway at the edge of the network of strings that sectioned off the dig. Her expression wasn't unfriendly, but she said, "Good morning, Harry. Please, be as quick and as brief as you can."

I held her eye a moment. "Always," I said. "Do you know who Danny was with before he died?"

She shrugged. "He was here, working. We had lunch and..." She shrugged again.

"Who'd he eat lunch with?"

She gave me that "are you crazy" look women reserve for questions like, "Where were you last night till four AM?" and "Who gave you that perfume?" I repeated the question by raising my eyebrows. She sighed. "Probably—I don't remember but usually he ate lunch with Charlie."

"Then can I talk to Charlie, please?"

She turned and I followed her to the edge of the dig. I counted eight kids, mostly girls, and a couple of guys, though there may have been more I couldn't see. Earl looked over from the far side of the dig, raised a hand briefly and looked away. Liz yelled:

"Charlie! Where's Charlie?"

Her voice didn't so much echo against the vast rocks as batter them. Everyone looked up from their work, then looked around searching for Charlie. Someone pointed to where the great wall curved away to the right and the ground dipped toward the valley. As they did so a waif of a girl with luminous platinum hair, very white skin and a straw hat appeared and waved a trowel.

Liz bellowed, "Charlie! Get over here!" Then she grinned at me. "You assumed Charlie was a boy, right?"

I regarded her face a moment without expression. "No, Liz, I instinctively knew this was one of those statistics-defying moments we all live for."

She snorted.

Charlie skipped once and broke into a run. For a moment I wondered if she might break with the effort, but she turned out to be tougher than she looked. By the time she arrived her cheeks were flushed and her eyes were all sparkly blue. She stared at me and then stared at Liz, like speaking was pointless.

"Charlie, this is Harry. He's investigating Danny's death. Answer his questions quickly and succinctly and get back to work. Be as cooperative as you can, we want him to leave as soon as possible."

Charlie said, "OK," and Liz went back to the dig.

Charlie said, "I am Karina." Then she pointed to some large rocks overlooking the valley nearby and said. "There are rocks. We can sit there." And then, like it was an explanation for both her name and the rocks, "I am Finnish."

"Good," I said. "Let's sit."

As we walked she said, "Did you know Danny?"

"No."

"I liked him. But now he is dead."

We sat, I on a smooth, round rock on the ground and she on a larger boulder, looking down at me. The early sun gleamed on her platinum hair. Her eyes were very blue.

"You spoke to him the day he died?"

"Yeah. We took lunch and he talked to me."

"What did he say?"

Her eyes widened slightly, but that was the only indication there was an expression going on there. "I cannot remember everything he said."

I gave her an empty smile. "That's disappointing. How about in general terms? What did you talk about?"

"He was a little bit not well. He had not much energy or motivation. He was without the list?"

"Listless?"

"Yuh. And when I ask him why, he tells me he does not know. But he is scared."

"What of?"

She leaned forward slightly and her very blue eyes opened wide.

"Ghosts!"

"He was afraid of ghosts? Are you sure?"

"This is what he told me. That he was afraid because Liz's dig is going to open the doors of the long tunnels."

"The long tunnels? Is that an Inca thing?"

She gave her head a small shake. "No. It is because the tunnels are very long, and go all the way down, down, down into the middle of the Earth, where is hell. Hell for Incas is called Ukupacha."

"And that's where the Supay live."

She smiled like I was sweet, with her head slightly on one side..

"There are three worlds in Inca mythology, Hananpacha, Kaypacha and Ukupacha. Heaven, Middle Earth and Under-world. Each one is separate, with physical borders, but also many connections." Her eyes opened wide again. "Physical and spiritual connections, passing between them like doors, and arches, and threads of the spider's web." She pointed a long, white finger up at the sky. "Lightning, light, rain and rainbows all come down from the sky and touch the Earth, connecting us with Hanan-pacha. Mountains rise up from inside the earth, reaching up from Kaypacha to the heavens. And caves and springs are the gateways from the Middle Earth, Kaypacha, into the world below, Ukupacha. Springs," she said again, "caves and of course, long tunnels. The gods and the daemons can also travel, by using these connections, from one pacha to another."

"And Danny believed that the Supay, the daemons from the underworld, were going to use the tunnels to rise up to the Middle Earth. What made him believe that?"

I saw her blue eyes drift over toward the dig. I knew what was going through her mind.

"Whatever you tell me stays between you and me. Dr. Calder will never hear about what you have told me. This is strictly confidential."

"Can you guarantee that?"

I sighed. "Of course not. But I can give you my word."

She echoed my sigh, but there was a touch of irony to hers. She pointed up at the towering mountain peak behind me. "This is Apusupay, it is like the sacred mountain of the daemons, and of the Daemon God, Supay. He is a daemon, but he is also many daemons. This is his mountain. The Inca sacrificed many children. Did you know that?"

An uncomfortable feeling crept into my belly and settled there. I shook my head. "No, I didn't know that."

If the emperor died, or his wife gave birth to a son, or if he was ill, or if they feared some natural disaster..." She paused, staring up at the massive peak. "Whenever the priests believed it was necessary for the gods or the daemons to intercede or be placated." She shifted her eyes to look at me. "This sacrifice was the ultimate link, the ultimate connection between the Middle Earth, Kaypacha, and the other two realms, Hananpacha and Ukupacha." Suddenly her blue eyes laughed, though her face remained almost expressionless. "It was like the Inca red telephone."

She stopped again and the laughter faded from her eyes. "Thousands of children might be sacrificed. The ceremony was called qhapaq ucha. It means 'the great, solemn crime.'"

SIX

WE SAT IN SILENCE FOR A TIME, WHILE I WATCHED THE morning breeze move her almost translucent hair, waiting for her to continue. Eventually she took a deep breath.

"There are no reliable, written records, but it seems the children were selected maybe a year before, boys and girls, and fed coca and alcohol, a little more every month, probably to subdue them and make them obedient. Then they were taken to high mountain temples, or sacred sites. The children were probably unconscious, and they were killed by strangulation, suffocation, sometimes a strong blow on the head. Or sometimes they were buried alive while they were unconscious. Other times they were left to die of cold."

She looked down at the ground between her feet. The breeze moved her hair and for a moment it looked like the halo of an angel. "The Mighty Crime," she said absently.

"This was a long time ago."

"Five hundred years."

"What has this to do with Danny Cooper?"

She hesitated—a lot—looking out over the valley that tumbled down to the vast, gleaming snake of the Urubamba flowing past the mountain.

"He told me," she said at last, "that..." Her eyes traveled past me and she made a small gesture with her chin, pointing toward the dig. "That she had told him she had made a discovery. When children were sacrificed to the gods they were fed for a year on coca and fermented maize, to bring peace to their souls, so that they would be embraced by Viracocha, god.

"But if it was necessary to appease Supay, then a different drug was used. They called it nuna miyu. It means something like 'soul poison.'"

A big bell went off in my memory. I quoted, "'Supay is coming in the tunnels and the deep caves... They will poison us, with nuna miyu, and then they will eat our souls.'"

She didn't react. She just said, "That is what Danny believed. He said that she had discovered this, and she was going to open the gate to Ukupacha and allow the Supay to emerge."

I gave her a hard stare. "Do you believe this bullshit?"

"No."

"But he did?"

"In the end, yes. He was obsessed. It was all he could think about. On the last day, we had lunch. Then, after, he went up the path to Apusupay. I never saw him again."

"You knew him better than anybody here, right?"

She gave a small shrug and tilted her head. "I am not so sure. He was intimate with Cas, and close also with..." She nudged her chin toward the dig.

"Dr. Calder?"

She kind of winced with her eyebrows, gave her head a small shake and said, "Shshsh..."

I laughed. "Has she got bionic hearing?"

"She can hear, if you say her name." I watched her hard for a moment, playing with an idea. She looked away. "I must get back to my work."

"Karina?"

"Yes."

"But they call you Charlie."

"Yes."

"Are you Carl Allen?"

A small frown, a tiny contraction of her brow. "No. I am Karina Aalto."

"Do you know Carl Allen? He was a friend of Danny's. Do you know who he is?"

"No."

"I don't believe you."

Still no expression. "OK."

"Look, Karina, Charlie, I am here to help you. I'm in room 1-A at Cas's hotel." I handed her a card with my number on it. "Call me, come and see me, if there is anything more you want to tell me that you don't feel comfortable telling me here and now."

She took the card and put it in her pocket. "There is nothing else."

I nodded. "OK, you can go."

I watched her walk away. She was like a Pre-Raphaelite painting, or something on an Art Nouveau lampshade. I shook my head to myself. That wasn't it. She was straight out of Tolkien, frail yet strong, and made out of pure light.

I grunted, got to my feet and followed her steps back to the dig. Dr. Calder was already there waiting for me when I arrived.

"Who's next?"

"You."

"Impossible. I'm working."

"Tell me about nuna miyu."

"What?"

Her eyes were shaded by the brim of her hat, but she narrowed them into a squint.

"Nuna miyu, soul poison. Tell me about it."

"It's a myth."

"You don't think so. You were closer with Danny than you let on and you told him about it. For some reason that freaked him out and you killed him."

"Is that something you can prove?"

"Not yet."

"Then go to hell!"

She turned and went to walk away, but stopped dead when I said, "But I don't need to prove it."

She turned slowly. "What's that supposed to mean?"

"I'm not arresting anyone. I'm not taking anybody home in handcuffs."

She studied my eyes very carefully, and I didn't hide what they were telling her. She retraced her two angry steps with more caution.

"The best interpretation I can put on that is that you can screw things up for me in DC."

"I don't give a damn what interpretation you put on it. I am telling you plainly that I am not here to take prisoners." I gave that a moment to sink in, then asked, "Is that why you got close to Danny? Because his family had influence in DC?"

"It's a dirty world. You know that better than anybody."

"What is nuna miyu?"

She muttered, "Over here."

I followed her across the expanse of dirt sectioned off with stakes and lines of string to an area where a large tent had been set up against the massive stones that formed the wall. She pushed open the flap and went in to the dim shade. I followed.

The tent was big, maybe twelve or fifteen feet across, not quite square, and everywhere there were wooden cases filled with artifacts; some partly wrapped in paper, others clearly visible. She sat in a director's chair on the far side of a trestle table littered with papers, small statues and bits of broken pottery. I sat opposite.

She said: "Nuna miyu was a myth. Every sacrificial child we ever found, including the Maiden at Llullaillaco, proved conclusively that they were given steadily increasing levels of coca and chicha, fermented corn. Those doses were sometimes massive on the day of the sacrifice."

"But...?"

She sighed and rubbed her face with hands that would have been fine and sensitive if they were not so calloused.

"But," she echoed with emphasis, giving a single nod. "There were Spanish accounts that suggested that coca and chicha were reserved for children who were to be sent to Hananpacha."

"The good place."

"If you like. Children who were to be sacrificed to Supay were given a different drug. The reasoning was, Viracocha, the god of Hananpacha, would take the children's souls to his bosom and care for them. But Supay had no such benign intentions. Supay wanted to eat the souls of the children. And so they were not given mind-altering drugs to open the gates of perception and allow free passage to the souls. They were given a different drug which killed their souls and rendered them defenseless against the daemons of Ukupacha."

I nodded. "OK, Liz, you and I both know that that is a lot of hogwash and superstitious bullshit. I doubt even the thirteen-year-old kids who were sacrificed believed it when the priests turned up with the mirrors and the credit cards."

"That's not funny."

"It wasn't meant to be. For the last time. What is nuna miyu? What did you tell Danny about nuna miyu that put him into a depression so bad he went up the hill and jumped off?"

She reached out her arms and gripped either end of the table, staring down at the chaos of papers and pottery in front of her.

"I don't honestly know. We had a conversation. We had had various. I am not ashamed to admit that I was cultivating him because I knew his father had influence in DC. We had made—I had made—a discovery which was shattering. This site was like no other anybody had ever seen." She gave a grim laugh and nodded several times at the table. "But I know what happens to archeologists who rock the boat and claim to have found evidence that alters the established view of history. They get buried. Sometimes literally."

"But you told Danny?"

"I managed to conceal it from everyone. I needed time to think before I came out and published what I had found. I needed political protection and allies back in DC and Boston. Randy Ortega is a good ally, but I needed more."

"But what had you found?"

She gave a small laugh, like she was listening to somebody else instead of me.

"And then Danny came along. I started grooming him and cultivating his interest. He had all these crazy ideas about how the Incas were what was left of Atlantis, and that they had been visited and helped by people from another planet. All that shit. So he was prime, ready for what I needed him to do."

"Liz, what had you found?"

"Iron."

"Iron? Is that such a big deal? They had gold, bronze, copper..."

"Iron was not known to the Incas. There is not a trace of it anywhere. The first recorded iron tool on Earth was in Mesopotamia, three thousand years BC. It started to arrive in Europe in the eleventh century before Christ."

I shrugged, getting irritated, and shook my head. "What are you trying to tell me, Liz?"

"Shortly after I started digging this place, I found a chamber, in the megalithic temple behind us."

"That massive wall?"

"Yes. I am deliberately not excavating it. I have placed my tent in front of the entrance. Because of what we might find—what I have already found. In that small chamber I found a cup—an iron cup. It had a residue in it: some resinous material caked with what appeared to be dried leaves and perhaps fruit."

"An infusion of some sort."

"Yes. So I took a small sample and sent it for radiocarbon dating. I said nothing about what it was or where it was found."

I waited. "And?"

"It came back that the contents of the cup were twelve thousand years old."

"That's impossible. It was a mistake."

"Obviously that was what I assumed. So I sent out three samples to three different labs, all highly reputable. The results all came back the same. They all dated the material, with a small margin of error, to twelve thousand years ago." She took a deep breath and leaned back in her chair. "The Inca Empire existed five hundred to a thousand years ago. To claim that there were Incas making megalithic temples in the Andes twelve thousand years ago would ruin my career. But to claim they were making tea in iron cups that long ago would finish me completely."

"Yeah." I nodded. "I can see that."

She reached into a box behind her and came out with a bottle of Johnny Walker Black Label and a couple of shot glasses. As she set them up I could see her hands were shaking.

"Coffee's behind you."

I turned and saw an old-fashioned red enamel coffee pot gently steaming on a double-ring propane portable stove. Beside it there was a tray with a cluster of cups and mugs. I took two espresso cups, filled them with hot black coffee and set them on the table. She was refilling her glass.

"History is not an account of our past. History is the backstory of who we believe ourselves to be. Our society has developed a very powerful backstory about how and why the West has become the dominant power in the world. History says it should be so, and archeology is the science that proves history is right. You try to change that picture at your peril, my friend."

I sipped the coffee and ran through what she was telling me. In the end I shrugged again.

"Yeah, everything you are saying makes sense. History has always been a political tool. But I am not seeing why Danny Cooper, on learning that the stuff in the iron cup was twelve thousand years old, would take himself to the top of Apusupay and jump off."

She knocked back the second shot, smacked her lips and sighed loudly.

"I already told you I don't know."

"Where is the cup now?"

"In an airtight, sealed box at a notary's office in Cusco. And no, the notary does not know what it is."

"How long ago did you have it dated?"

"About a year ago, during the initial dig."

I watched her for a while. She knew what the next question was going to be and she was avoiding my eye. Finally I asked her.

"Did you ever have the stuff analyzed?"

A pause, then, "No."

"You're lying."

Suddenly she was fierce. Her teeth were clenched and her neck was corded with tendons. "This cannot go beyond this conversation!"

"It doesn't need to if you cooperate with me."

She leaned forward, her elbows on the table and her eyes boring into mine.

"I need their help!"

"What was in the cup?"

She stared at me and swallowed three times before answering.

"I sent it to three highly reputable labs. They all agreed it was a combination of leaves and fruit which were unknown."

"Unrecognizable...?"

"No, not unrecognizable, unknown. As in extinct, never discovered, never seen before."

"And you think it's nuna miyu."

"It's possible."

We sat in silence for a while. Bright strips of sunlight filtered in through the flaps of the tent. Distant birdsong was overlaid by the desultory sounds of the dig: a voice calling, a faintly echoed laugh, the soft, irregular scraping of trowels.

"What did you talk about that day?"

"I told him I needed his help."

"To do what?"

"Isn't it obvious? I was sitting on one of the most significant archeological finds of the last three centuries. I could become one of the great, iconic names in archeology. Or I could sink without a trace and be written off and forgotten forever, along with this site. What I needed was the political clout of Danny's family. I needed somebody to pull strings, big strings, so that when I presented my findings they would be supported and backed by eminent names."

"So you wanted him to talk to his father."

"Edwin Cooper, of Cooper Aerospace, a billionaire scientist with a lot of clout on the Hill and in the White House. The family have a tradition of supporting the arts and being pretty broadminded."

"What did he say?"

"He said he'd call his father and talk to him. If his dad was receptive he'd fly back and arrange for a meet between the three of us. Obviously I told Danny he would get a lot of credit for the find..." She shrugged like she didn't like the taste she was giving herself in her mouth. "Politics."

I leaned back in my chair and rubbed my face.

"So you told him if he helped you out you would share the credit on one of the most important archeological finds of the last three hundred years. He tells you you've got a deal, he climbs into one of the Jeeps, goes to the top of Apusupay and jumps off."

She stared into her empty glass. Her coffee was untouched, going cold.

"Yeah," she said, and reached for the bottle. "That's about the size of it."

SEVEN

I LEFT HER IN HER TENT, SCOWLING AT HER WHISKY. I crossed the esplanade among the hunched archeologists in denim shorts and straw hats scratching away at the dust, searching for the broken remains of a society that had believed it was the solemn duty of the state to commit the solemn crime of doping and killing children.

The state's solemn duty to commit a solemn crime. The Ministry of Solemn Crimes. Funny how a society could be Orwellian five hundred years before Orwell was born. I raised an eyebrow at myself. At least what I did was illegal.

I followed the path of broad shallow steps that skirted the vast wall. Danny Cooper had followed this same path. My footsteps were overlapping his, separated only by six months in time. He had, minutes before, agreed to talk to his father on Dr. Calder's behalf. It was a move that was going to make his name as an archeologist.

I reached the top of the steps to the area of flatland where the trucks were parked. He had reached this same spot. Had he already decided to take his life? Or did something else happen here? Did he meet someone? Did someone come with him from the dig? Whatever it was, he had climbed into the Jeep and, instead of heading back down the hill, he had gone up, grinding through the gears, following what was little more than a goat track, for another three or four miles, to his death.

I climbed in the Land Rover, fired up the big V8 and did that same thing, grinding slowly up the path that followed the spine of the mountain. It meandered through forests where the cries and screeches of the birds echoed, deafening in the dark, then broke out again into bright sunshine, where green meadows fell away steeply to left and right, before winding through a narrow gorge and climbing steeply again toward the peak.

It took me a full half hour to reach the summit. The summit was not a sharp peak, but rather an expanse, maybe fifty yards square, of softly undulating grassland. The air was thin. It was thin down in San Julian, but up here it felt like a mild strain on your lungs. There was not much oxygen in the air, and a small amount of exercise made you feel light-headed. I wondered if that had happened to Danny. He had come here to think. He got too close to the edge, became light-headed...

But I dismissed the idea as soon as it came to me. He had been here long enough to become acclimatized. He had worked every day at the dig, at these altitudes. He had adjusted and become accustomed.

I stood a while. The view was extraordinary. I was looking down into deep, narrow ravines, tangled and overgrown with trees and vines I could not identify. Small clouds of mist trailed among the canopy, and also higher, among the peaks. Far, far below I could see the Urubamba, broad and deep, weaving among sandbanks and steep, sheer mountain walls.

The story was he had jumped down into the river. But looking around I saw that wasn't easy to do. There were shelves and outcrops and steep slopes everywhere. What I could not find was a sheer drop. I approached the edge and looked down. If I had jumped from there I would almost certainly break my back and my neck, but I would be caught and stopped by the trees long before I hit the water.

Scanning the area I realized that if I wanted to hit the river, I would need to walk almost half a mile, scramble down a ledge, walk another hundred yards and then jump. So if Danny was found in the Urubamba River, that was where he jumped from. He had parked the Jeep and, in this thin, enervating atmosphere, he had walked over half a mile to a spot where he could be sure of falling into the river.

It didn't make a lot of sense.

I turned and looked back toward where I had left the truck, a few paces from the highest point. If I wasn't fussy about hitting the river, and I couldn't imagine why anybody would be, if I just wanted to kill myself, a jump from that point, down the south face, would give me a thousand yards of drop before I hit anything. So the question was obvious. Why go to all the trouble of scrambling down half a mile to jump into the river, when he could kill himself right here?

The answer was equally simple. He was, as Carl Allen had implied in his letter, murdered. And he wound up falling from that spot after either a fight or a chase.

So now the question was, if he was killed, what was he killed for? What benefit did the killer get from throwing Danny Cooper, Edwin Cooper's son, off Apusupay and into the Urubamba River?

I made my way across the open land back toward the Land Rover. There was a large boulder, partly covered by yellow moss, with smaller boulders clustered at its base. I found one that looked more or less flat and sat, looking down the track toward the dig, three or four miles away, and the deep, tangled green gorge to the right, which led eventually, by wending ways, to the great river before it turned south at Quillabamba.

Down there, invisible among that miasma of trees, bushes, creepers and exotic plants, not to mention the exotic multi-legged creatures, was the equally exotic Dr. Amanda Epstein. I wondered about her for a moment. Dr. Calder had said anyone might easily fall in love with her. I tried to recall her exact words. I closed my eyes and went back in my mind to the hotel. Liz Calder was sitting across from me with the bottle of Scotch and her shot glass. She'd said:

"Danny was twenty-four going on fourteen. He was real excited about being selected for the dig." Then she'd said something about his being childishly excited—something like that— and having met two women. "Dr. Amanda Epstein, who any man or woman would have to be blind or deaf not to fall in love with. I might well be in love with her myself if I paid any attention to her. And Cas, who is probably also very easy to fall in love with." And her last words, "So Danny, being a total schmuck, fell in love with them both."

There were tenuous threads that seemed to link the exotic Epstein and the not so exotic Calder. But they were gossamer and when you tried to grasp them they evaporated.

I opened my eyes and about half a mile away I saw an off-white Wrangler bumping and lurching its way up the track toward me. It was raising dust and the morning sun was reflecting off the windshield, so it was hard to make out any details of the driver. After a couple of minutes the truck rolled to a halt beside the Land Rover and the driver climbed down.

I didn't know him. He was about six foot, lean, in khaki chinos and a pale, linen jacket. He had short, dark hair, slightly balding, and dark shades over his eyes. I watched him as he walked toward me.

"Henry Baumb?"

"Who's asking?"

"Don Gardner, Office of Internal Accounting at the Pentagon."

"You came all the way from Virginia?"

"I have an urgent message that needs to be delivered personally. Are you Henry Baumb?"

"I guess that depends on the message."

"I'm going to take that as a yes."

He said it as he reached inside his jacket, but I was already running at him. Two sprinting strides and I collided with him, pinning his right hand to his chest with my left hand and driving my right fist into his floating ribs. We crashed in a tangled mess on the ground. He was wheezing but he wasn't finished. He was still struggling to get his weapon free and clawing at my face with his left hand. I scrambled to get into a sitting position on top of him, landed a right cross on his face that didn't do much, and he squirmed and twisted, rolling on his side. I began to fall to the side, losing my grip on his wrist. The weapon came free and I saw the madness in his eyes as he wrenched the semiautomatic from its holster and waved it an inch from my face.

I smacked the cannon with my left hand as I fell, and grasped at it frantically at the same time. He was struggling to get to his feet, grasping the butt with both hands and levering it toward me. I was still on my side in the dirt, gripping the cannon with one hand, trying frantically to keep it pointed away from me.

I drew up my right knee and with my right hand grabbed at my ankle. I found the Fairbairn and Sykes and pulled it from my ankle scabbard. I saw his eyes swivel and take in the blade. He gritted his teeth and leaned on the gun with all his weight, but it was too late. I rammed the razor-sharp steel into his forearm and twisted for good measure. His scream echoed out across the mountains like a wounded ghost, and he let go of the gun. I yanked out the blade and he staggered back, gripping his arm and groaning spasmodically. I thrust his pistol in my waistband behind my back and went after him.

He panicked and ran. He went toward the boulder like he thought he might find refuge there. I shouted, "Wait! I don't want to hurt you! I just want to talk!"

It sounded lame even to me. He ran, staggering, leaving a thick trail of blood. He wasn't going very far. I put the blade back in the scabbard and ran, calling, "Wait up, will you! I only need you to answer some questions! You were just doing your job, for Christ's sake!"

He'd reached the boulder and stopped, wheezing badly and

looking back at me with fear in his eyes. I stopped dead and held up both hands.

"All I want is to know who and why. Keep running and I'll catch you, and then I'll have to hurt you. Talk to me and you can go home. You mean nothing to me. You're just an employee, right?"

He didn't say anything, but his eyes said he was listening, searching for hope.

"Just tell me who sent you, and why. I'll get in my Land Rover and leave, and you go look for a doctor."

He turned and stepped toward me. He was very pale. I could see beads of sweat on his brow, and he was starting to tremble, like he was freezing cold. He was going into shock. If I wanted something from him, it had to be now.

"I don't know why," he said. "They just told me you had to die. You must not finish this job."

He took another step and I moved toward him. "Who?" I said, "Who gave you the contract?"

"Cusco, Cusco field office..."

He lurched and as he lurched he lunged. It was a stiletto with a five-inch blade. He was slow and telegraphed the lunge long before it came. I took his arm, folded it behind his back and frog-marched him to the edge of the cliff. There I stopped, half a mile above the forest that would tear him to shreds when he got there. I held him suspended and trembling.

"Did you kill Danny Cooper?"

"No."

"Who sent you?"

"Cusco. They have a temporary field office in Cusco."

"Who?"

He turned his head, staring at me crazily from the corner of his eye, his face almost touching mine. "Cobra!"

He wrenched himself free, turned, trying to grab at me, but lost his footing and suddenly he was leaning back, teetering and he was gone. There was no long scream echoing among the peaks, just his body hurtling down the sheer face until it plunged in among the canopy of trees.

Henry.

I turned and walked away toward my vehicle.

Henry.

I was trying to remember who knew me as Henry. Everyone I had introduced myself to knew me as Harry. Henry would be the brigadier, the colonel and Senator Randy Ortega. Or one of a very small number of people they might have spoken to. One or two, no more.

I climbed in the Land Rover and drove slowly down to San Julian. As I drove past the dig I slowed and watched to see if anyone looked up or looked surprised. Nobody did, so I kept on going.

I parked outside Angie's Hostal and walked into the quiet, peaceful gloom of the bar. Cas wasn't there yet so I spoke to the girl behind the bar.

"You have a telephone I can use? My cell has no reception here."

"Sure, round the corner you got a little booth."

I followed the direction of her finger and found a wooden booth with a curtain and what must have been an Inca telephone with a revolving dial. I left the little blue curtain open so I could see who was listening, and sat on the bentwood chair provided. The phone rang twice and the brigadier came on the line.

"You're calling from a landline."

"I'm in the Andes, sweetheart. Signal's not great up here. I understand the Inca satellites all stopped working about twelve thousand years ago."

He was very quiet for a moment, so I added, "Are you surprised to hear from me?"

"Should I be? You're not making a lot of sense at the moment."

"Your friend from Cusco came to talk to me."

"Really?"

"At first he couldn't find me because everybody here calls me Harry, and he was asking for Henry. Only people who call me Henry are you and your wife and a couple of your friends."

"But you spoke to him and the chat went well."

"Yeah, his mind is at rest."

"Super. Well, look, your minute's up. I hear Cusco is nice for a day trip. Cheerio!"

And he was gone. It had been less than a minute, but a minute was as long as he was prepared to stay on an unsecured line. The suggestion of a daytrip to Cusco was if I had any more to say, I should use my secure cell or a public phone in the city. But I'd told him all I needed to tell him. There was a leak. And the pool of suspects was very small.

I didn't think the brigadier or the colonel had sent this hit man. They were too smart and they knew me too well to send one guy armed with a semiautomatic. Which left the senator, or somebody the senator had spoken to. His crack about my nickname suggested he had spoken to a couple of people at least. But about what exactly, and how much he had given away was hard to tell.

For now it would have to be the brigadier's problem. I had a different problem: How does a twelve-thousand-year-old iron cup lead to crimes against humanity?

I looked at my watch. It was lunchtime and I went through to the bar to order a hamburger and a cold beer, thinking that by the looks of it the iron cup had been directly involved, as an instrument, in crimes against humanity—a hundred and twenty centuries ago. Now, on the say-so of a crazy person going by the name of Carl Allen, the brigadier and a senator of the United States Congress were willing to believe that crimes against humanity were either being perpetrated again, or were about to be. But who was doing it, and how, was for me to find out.

I leaned on the bar, gave my order and went out to sit in the early afternoon sunshine.

It was too improbable. The whole thing was too improbable. Which meant that either the brigadier had agreed, in exchange for continued funding, to have me hunt down Danny's killer on the pretext of there being a major crime concealed behind Danny's murder, or...

My mind trailed off, staring up at the massive peak of Apusupay looming over the tiny town of San Julian.

Or the brigadier knew something he wasn't willing to tell me, and he was playing his usual, subtle game with his cards close to his chest. There was something. There was something. I could feel it. Something in the relationship between Dr. Liz Calder and Danny, Liz Calder and Dr. Amanda Epstein, Dr. Liz Calder and Cas. She was at the center, like a spider, with her iron bowl, with Danny bound up in her sticky threads.

A shadow fell across my thoughts and I looked up to see a woman blocking out the sun. She was the kind of woman it would be very, very easy to fall hopelessly in love with.

EIGHT

"Do you mind if I join you?"

I smiled, and after a moment I stood. "You must be Dr. Epstein."

She laughed. "Is it that obvious?"

"The person who described you nailed it." I gestured at the chair she was holding. "Please. Will you have a drink?"

She sat. "Sparkling water, with ice and lemon."

I sat too and called the waitress. I gave her the order and when she went away Epstein leaned forward slightly and smiled. She didn't look like a woman who had just spent a couple of years sleeping with millipedes. She looked fresh, well groomed and her fingernails were clean and well trimmed.

"I hope I am not intruding. I heard you were a private investigator looking into Danny's death, and I thought I'd come to you before you came to me. By the way, I'd be grateful if you called me Amanda rather than Dr. Epstein. May I call you Harry? Or do you prefer Henry? Or Mr. Baumb?"

It was obviously rehearsed, but well delivered. I waited till she'd finished, gave it a moment and then asked her, "What makes you think I was going to talk to you?"

She frowned a little. "Oh, really? Because I am sure you have heard by now, from at least one source, that Danny and I were close."

"I heard he was desperately in love with you. I also heard that anyone in their right senses would be."

She threw back her head and laughed. It could have looked affected, but it wasn't. "Who on Earth told you that?"

I ignored the question. "So how close were you and Danny?"

She sat back in her chair and gestured around her with both hands.

"Look around you. Small towns are small towns, whether it's in New Mexico, Iowa, France or Afghanistan—or a million miles from anywhere in the Andes. And you can't get much more small and remote than San Julian. Danny was charming, well-educated, a real gentleman. He was also a good ten years younger than me, very naïve and unworldly. But, he was refreshing."

I nodded like I understood. "Sure," I said, "but that tells me why you were close, which I had pretty much figured out already. What it doesn't tell me is what I asked you, how close you were."

She regarded me for a moment from under an arched eyebrow.

"You're not very naïve and unworldly, are you, Harry?"

"I used to be. Then I met a woman you couldn't help falling in love with."

"Something tells me she was the midwife who delivered you."

"Are you going to tell me or do I need to tickle you into submission? You asked to join me, remember?"

The waitress brought the sparkling water and my beer. When she'd gone Amanda Epstein sat a while turning her glass around, watching the bubbles cling to the side of the glass, then lose their grip, rise to the top and become one with the air. Eventually she took a deep breath.

"I am embarrassed to admit that I was actually in love with him, Harry, but I was."

That I was not expecting and my arched eyebrow said so.

"See?" she said, "That is exactly the reaction I expected. It is how everyone and anyone would react. And no, I don't have a thing about younger men. It was just him. He was special. He was kind, enthusiastic, full of life, intelligent, believed everything was possible. He offered me a view of life I had never believed possible before."

"So... How close were you, Amanda?"

"Very close. Intimate. We were lovers, briefly."

I took a sip of my beer and spoke as I set it down.

"Here's the thing. People keep telling me how naïve and innocent Danny was. But, and I hope you'll forgive me for saying this, in his naïve innocence it seems he was having affairs with at least two women, simultaneously, possibly more."

She gave a small laugh. "Well, in a town like this, when you look like Danny... But it wasn't simultaneous. Shortly after he arrived Danny let me know how he felt. It is my extreme ill fortune, Harry, that men do seem to be attracted to me. I don't look for it, but it's there. What I have got into the habit of doing is dismissing men who come on to me, automatically. I am, if you will forgive the cliché, wedded to my work. And when I dismissed Danny I didn't give it a second thought."

"So what happened?"

"Cas happened. Cas is a very attractive woman, if she only knew it, but unlike me she is very open to the approaches attractive men make to her. She liked Danny a lot, she came on to him a lot, and he went for it hook, line and sinker. And as I watched, I began to feel jealous. Then I noticed even Liz, the Iron Lady, was putting the moves on him. So I thought, the hell with it! And I let him know if he approached me again I might be more receptive. He did, and I was. We were together three times, and then he died."

The waitress brought out my hamburger and I asked her for another beer. Amanda smiled at the waitress and pointed at my plate. "Can I have one of those too?"

When the waitress had gone I said, "What was that, a week?"

She looked amused. "A little more. About two weeks."

I picked up a piece of lettuce and looked at it for a second before putting it in my mouth.

"Who's Carl Allen?"

She frowned. "Carl Allen?" I nodded and chewed, watching her, trying to read her expression and see if it was fake. "I don't know anyone here called Carl Allen."

"How about Carlos Allende?"

"No."

"What are you doing at your site? Would you object to my going to see it?"

I phrased it carefully, like I was asking for an invitation, but I was going to go see it anyway; all I really wanted to know was whether she would object. The small frown and the slight narrowing of her eyes said she was a little offended.

"I have no objection at all to your visiting the site, but I warn you it is nothing like Liz's dig. It's the three Ds: deep, dark and damp. And if you don't like creepy little bugs and animals, this is not the place for you."

I paused a moment to pick up another piece of lettuce.

"When I was in the rainforest in Colombia we used to eat creepy little bugs and animals to stay alive. They have two great advantages, they are very high in protein, and you don't have to bury the wrappers."

She was quiet for a long while. She'd got the obvious message that I had been in special operations. I wasn't sure if I had over-played my hand or not, but I had sniffed in every corner of San Julian and all I could find was that Danny was connected, everybody loved Danny, Danny loved everybody and his hormones had killed him. I needed to start rattling cages, and I was interested in Amanda Epstein's cage. Eventually she made a little shrug with her eyebrows.

"I see," she said. "Well, in that case you'll have no objection to the site. What am I doing there? I am under contract to the Pasqüal Pharmaceutical Company of Munich to carry out research. I don't know whether you are aware of it, Harry, but

Peru has the richest biodiversity in the world, more even that the Amazon Basin. Cool air comes up from the Antarctic, along the Pacific coast..."

"I know," I cut in, "and interacts every few years with the warm, moist air from El Niño, creating a uniquely rich ecosystem. I have done my homework. What I actually asked you was what you were doing there, not for whom, what."

She shook her head. "You know perfectly well that that information is confidential."

"You told me a while ago that I was neither naïve nor unworldly, and you were right. I like you, I think you're very attractive and I can see why people fall for you..." I let the ambiguity of the term hang. "But a young man died, in very peculiar circumstances, a young man you claim to have been in love with, and the information I have indicates that his death was just the tip of a very ugly iceberg. So, as you can imagine, I am not just going to shrug my shoulders and say, 'Oh well, that information is confidential, never mind!'"

The sadness returned to her eyes. I had expected a reaction: anger, hostility, defiance—but not sadness.

"What are you going to do, Harry?"

"Nothing, I hope. Because I hope you are going to see sense, take me up there and show me what you're doing. If you don't, I have several options. One of them, the least problematic for you, is that I arrange for any one of a number of US Departments to lean on the Peruvian cops to move in and raid your lab, your hotel, and anything else where you might keep data, including any and all of your computers. If the Pasqüal Pharmaceutical Company has offices in the States we can raid them too. I don't know what we'll find, but I reckon there is a damn good chance that next year there will be five or six more field labs in this valley than are there now."

She took a deep breath and sighed. "Neither naïve nor unworldly." She shook her head. "What you are is utterly ruthless."

"Yes, Amanda, especially when I suspect a serious crime is being committed."

"You're not a private investigator."

"That's irrelevant. I said that leaning on the cops here was the very least of what I could do. Be smart. Show me your field lab and explain to me what you are doing. It need never go beyond you and me. I am not in the pharmaceutical business. I have no interest in stealing your research."

Her expression didn't change. She stared at me for a long moment, impassive, and finally said, "You have no idea what my research is; how can you know whether you have an interest in stealing it?"

"Make your choice, Amanda. One way or another I am going to see that research. Let's do it in the way that impacts you and your work the least."

The waitress brought out her burger, set it in front of her and left. She sat staring at it and nodding slowly. Eventually she said, "Fine, this afternoon. Are you free? About three o'clock."

"Sure. Who else will be there?"

"I have five assistants who work with me. They'll be there."

"Male or female?"

Her expression became incredulous and suddenly she burst out laughing. As the laughter died away she frowned and narrowed her eyes.

"What kind of world do you live in, Harry? What do you think? You think I am going to lure you to my lab in the middle of the jungle and kill you?"

"No," I shook my head, "I don't think you are going to do that, Amanda. But I am aware that it is one of a number of possibilities."

"That's ridiculous."

"It's also ridiculous to suggest that Danny Cooper committed suicide. In fact, I know as a certainty that he didn't. I know for a fact that he was murdered. He was murdered because of what he knew and what he was going to tell his father."

She snorted. "Oh, come on! You've been reading too many…"

"They tried to kill me today."

She stopped dead. "What? Who did? Who's 'they'?"

"He followed me up to the top of Apusupay in a Jeep and tried to shoot me."

"Come on! You can't be serious!" She looked around in an exaggerated manner, spreading her hands, scoffing. "Where is this man now? Where is his Jeep?"

I was having trouble deciding if the act was genuine or theatrics. I spoke quietly.

"His Jeep is still at the top of Apusupay. He is about halfway down the south face, among the trees, a little bit broken."

She went very pale. That is something you can't fake. It's a reaction of the autonomic system. She spoke in a hoarse whisper.

"You…"

"I killed him. It's what I usually do to people who try to kill me. If you are going to keep scoffing and saying, 'Oh, come on,' I will take you up to see the Jeep and the woods."

"My god, who are you?"

I sat forward and gave her my most soulless smile. "Somebody you don't want to make the mistake of thinking is naïve or unworldly. I like you, Amanda, and maybe your whole beautiful person act is genuine and for real. But one way or another, I get to see what goes on at your lab." I pointed at her burger. "Are you going to eat that?"

She frowned at me a moment and then down at the burger, like I had suddenly spoken to her in ancient Greek. She shook her head. "No, not after what you have just told me."

She gathered her things and stood as I pulled her plate over. Before she turned to go I said, "I'll expect you at three."

"Yes, at three."

I bit into her burger and watched her walk away, wondering whether I had just been a total asshole to a lovely woman who didn't deserve it. Was she too good to be true, or was she just good —a really nice person it was easy to fall in love with? Either way, whatever she was, she didn't strike me as a new, sexy take on Dr. Mengele. I didn't see her committing crimes against humanity anytime soon.

But then, like Freud said, women are the dark continent, and nobody understands them.

I took another bite of her burger and sat chewing it, staring at the immense, almost vertical forested slopes that loomed over the town. The fact was, I hadn't found anyone in San Julian who struck me as likely to commit crimes against humanity anytime soon.

And yet.

There was a tenuous thread that led more or less directly from Dr. Amanda Epstein to Dr. Liz Calder and right back through the centuries to Incas who slaughtered thousands of children after doping them on cocaine and booze, in the name of their gods.

And their daemons.

Dr. Liz Calder, with her iron cup and her twelve-thousand-year-old mind-altering drug.

And then there were two inescapable facts: one, somebody had killed Danny Cooper; two, somebody had tried to kill me—here and in DC. It was a reasonable inference that Danny's murder and my attempted murders were attempts to keep a secret hidden. And that got me to thinking about Carl Allen, or Carlos Allende, as well hidden as the secret he was trying to bring to light. I needed to find him. Because I was running out of options. I had no doubt something dark was going down in San Julian, and I suspected it was in fact building toward some kind of atrocity, but I was as damned as the Supay if I had any idea what it was, or how to unearth it.

NINE

SHE CAME FOR ME AT TEN TO THREE. I HAD ALREADY showered and changed and was having coffee on the terrace. She was in an old, white Cherokee. As she pulled up beside the hotel terrace she lowered the window and leaned across the seat to speak to me.

"You want to ride with me?"

It was a bad idea for several reasons, all of which I ignored because my instinct told me if I went with the offer I would learn something. I pulled open the door and climbed in, clunking the door closed behind me.

"How do I get back?" I asked as we pulled away around the town square and out onto the Chancomayo Road. She grinned.

"Don't worry. I'll bring you back in one piece."

She seemed to have recovered from the shock of discovering that I had eaten bugs in the Colombian jungle.

"Before we go to your field lab I'd like to take a detour."

"I thought you might. To the top of Apusupay?"

"Mm-hmm, that OK?"

"As long as you're not going to ask me to look at any dead bodies."

"No."

Two minutes outside San Julian we came to an intersection of broad, dirt tracks. To the right the path led up south toward the dig, the top of the mountain and Amanda's field lab. She slowed and spun the wheel, and we started to climb. East, and across the ravine I could see the tangle of trees, bushes and vines, dark and impenetrable.

"How do you get in there?"

She was silent so long I thought she wasn't going to answer and glanced at her. She sighed.

"There was an old path—the remains of an old path, paved. That was how we found the place originally."

I frowned, I didn't get it. "You found the place to perform your research by following an old, paved path? How?"

"We'd heard..." She stopped, then started again. "This valley has a unique microclimate. We'd heard from local shamen—" She gave her head a rapid shake. "Actually, shaman is totally inappropriate. Shaman, or saman, is a Siberian word from the Tungus people who inhabit an area of eastern Siberia around the Tunguska River. It means simply 'one who knows.' Here in Peru we would talk about a paqu yachaq, what used to be called a witch doctor..."

"Amanda?"

She sighed again and nodded. "Yes, I know, I'm rambling again. So, several paqu yachaq in this part of the Sacred Valley told us that there were plants with great curative powers that grew only in this part of the Apusupay Valley. That is what this canyon is called. So Pasqüal became interested and asked me to investigate."

"Pasqüal, you make it sound like a person."

"It is a person. Very much so. Pasqüal Bouc is the founder of the Pasqüal Pharmaceutical Company of Munich. He holds a fifty-one percent share of the company and he is rapidly turning it into one of the five most important and innovative brands in the industry."

"And you're on first-name terms."

"Yes, we are very close."

"As close as you were with Danny?"

It slipped out and I almost regretted it, but she answered without blinking.

"Closer." Then she looked at me and raised an eyebrow. "Is that relevant?"

We had come to a fork in the track. The right fork was the one I had taken to go to the peak. The left fork wound down the steep slope toward the forest at the bottom of the ravine. She slowed and pointed.

"Down there, you can't see it from here, but there is a partially paved path that leads in through the trees."

We started moving again, climbing, whining in low gear, lurching over rocks and potholes.

"So what makes Pasqüal Bouc so special and innovative?"

She smiled a sly smile without looking at me. "You sound jealous."

"Maybe I am."

"Well, one of the things that makes him special is that he does not get jealous."

"Do you give him cause?"

"You know that I do. But I am a free spirit, Harry, and he respects that."

"Then he's a fool. Now, leaving sex aside, what makes him so innovative and special?"

She went quiet again and didn't answer until we were practically at the top of the mountain. There was a wooded crest, a hump in the path, and I knew that beyond it the cream Wrangler would become visible. Then she spoke suddenly.

"Pasqüal was also the founder of Nouvelle Vision."

"Sounds like a French TV channel."

"It's not." She slowed, crawling along the path as she spoke. "It's an association of companies within the chemical and pharmaceutical industries who are seeking to transform the way things are done, to make them greener, more respectful of the environment and more sustainable."

"And that's why you've spent the last year or two sitting in a shack in a canyon in darkest Peru, distilling beetle juice and grinding up unique leaves to see what chemicals they have in them."

"You sound sardonic, but basically the answer is yes. We could have spent two years synthesizing this stuff in labs in Geneva, but instead we have deepened our understanding of life on this planet, deepened our understanding of Peru's ecosystems, and the people who depend on them. I think they are all good things."

We crested the hill and came out of the trees and there, a few yards from the boulder, was the Wrangler, gleaming in the afternoon sun.

"So you," I said, "are not so much a pharmacologist as an anthrapharmacologist."

She was staring at the Jeep, crawling at barely four miles an hour.

"I don't know what you mean," she said, without taking her eyes from the truck.

"I mean that you, following Pasqüal's ethos, are not just studying the plants and bugs in this ravine, but their place in the socio-ecological dynamics of the people who inhabit this area," I spread my hands and pulled down the corners of my mouth, "the Inca, the post-Inca and the proto-Inca."

"I'm sorry, I have absolutely no idea what you're talking about."

I didn't answer her. She accelerated and after a minute we pulled up beside the Wrangler and she got out. I followed and joined her beside the hood of the Jeep, though she'd stopped looking at it and was now gazing out across the mountains.

"So it's true."

I pointed at the boulder. "I was sitting there. He pulled a gun on me."

"He pulled a gun on you, but he died."

"It happens more often than you might think." I took her elbow and led her to the edge of the sheer drop. She looked down the vertiginous, sheer face of the cliff at the fringe of the trees two thousand feet below. "He's in among the trees," I told her. "Did you know him?"

"Of course not."

"Did your husband send him?"

She frowned, but didn't look at me, staring down at the trees that held death in their shadows. "Why would you ask that?"

"Pasqüal Bouc is your husband, isn't he?"

"Was it that obvious?"

"Did he send him?"

"No, Pasqüal doesn't kill people. He saves lives."

"How about theft? Does he steal things?"

"I don't know what you're talking about," she said again, and now she looked up into my face. Her chest was rising and falling quickly. "Are you going to kill me too?"

"No. You can't give me what I want if you're dead."

Her voice was thick when she asked, "What do you want from me?"

"I want the nuna miyu."

She gave a small, involuntary gasp. "You know...?"

"Come on." I pulled her back a step. "Let's go see your lab."

We drove back along the track in silence. At the fork she slowed and turned right and we began to trundle slowly down the slope toward the rich, green jungle. We crossed a broad stream over a rickety wooden bridge and after that the ground leveled off and all around the trees and ferns became suddenly thick, reaching above the Cherokee and at times blocking out the light.

Ahead of us the sheer face of the mountain reared up and I saw that the cliff face formed a sharp right angle with the left, southern face making a wedge shape to the floor of the canyon, and the wall facing us forming what appeared at first to be a flat, perfectly square wall, about five hundred feet high and another five hundred across. But as we closed in on it I realized it was not a wall at all, but a vast cave with a gigantic, yawning maw about two or three hundred feet high, which was completely overgrown with dangling vines.

As we drew closer she slowed and the forest, towering fifteen or twenty feet above our heads, closed in, turning what little sunlight filtered through a liquid green. And now I saw that a path, about five or six feet across, had been cleared and laid with flat, irregular stones. This path curved its way in among the trees and we, crawling at three or four miles an hour, followed it toward the vast opening of the cave.

We hit the wall of dangling ivy, lianas and vines and I could not help wincing. But they parted and we passed through. And in a fraction of a second, everything had changed.

We were inside what amounted to a natural cathedral. The domed ceiling was lost to sight above, but every sound we made was hurled up there and batted around until echo mixed with echo, causing reverberations and tones that filled the cave with a chaos of lifeless ghosts.

The floor of this immense cave was bizarrely flat and shiny. It appeared to be vitrified with a high-gloss finish. The walls were irregular, and curved up into the shadows above. Ahead of us a semicircle of five large, military-style campaign tents had been set up, each about fifteen or twenty feet long, a good eight feet high and eight or ten feet deep. We climbed out of the truck and the slam of the doors resonated high up in the dome. I stared down at the perfect, smooth black floor.

"A freak of nature," she said. "Some bizarre result of volcanic activity. The rock must have been exposed to intense heat which liquefied and vitrified it. Gravity did the rest, leaving it almost smooth."

I pointed at the tents. "These are labs?" She nodded. I said, "That's at least seven to eight hundred square feet of equipment. That's a lot of lab."

"Eight hundred square feet. We have very limited access to the web, but we have pretty much everything we need right here.

Occasionally we deploy a satellite dish up on the mountain if we need to connect urgently with Munich. But that's not very often."

Inside, through the plastic windows, I could see people moving about. "What are they doing?"

"I'll show you, but you'll need to suit up."

She led me to the tent on the far left. Suiting up involved pulling on some latex gloves and covering my face with a mask and some goggles. Then she led me to the second tent, where three guys looked up from what they were doing and then decided to ignore us. I had no idea what they were about, but I could see there was a lot of very sophisticated equipment and they seemed to be processing plants and fruits which lay in plastic trays.

Amanda said, "We select plants and fruits from the forest outside, which we have sectioned into quadrants. We are moving through those quadrants systematically, identifying plants which are not known. So far we have identified fifteen new, unknown species of plant, and seven new types of fruit." She paused to look into my face. "Naturally occurring plants cannot be patented. You can only patent genetically engineered plants, or new plants discovered in a cultivated area. So it is very important that this area is kept strictly confidential."

"So you are analyzing these new plants you've discovered."

"To see their composition, and if there is any way is which they can be useful medically. The paqu yachaq in this area claim there are plants here which have remarkable medicinal properties, and that is what we are looking for."

"And when you find them?"

"Pasqüal believes in ethical business. This means he needs to make back his investment, and after that he makes the formula available to the market so that it can be made available to the world at the lowest price possible."

We stepped out of the tent and moved toward the next one. In through the flap we saw two more guys with masks, goggles and latex gloves. They also ignored us. Here they seemed to be using spectroscopes and centrifuges which were connected to computers and monitors.

"This is your full team. What's in the other tents?"

"We take the plants through a broad series of tests, analyzing them and their contents. They would be impossible to explain to a layperson. But in any case, today we are working here, in these two labs."

"Up on the mountain I told you I wanted the nuna miyu. You were shocked and said, 'You know...?' Tell me about nuna miyu."

The two assistants now turned and looked first at me and then at Epstein. She took my arm and led me out of the tent, across the black, echoing cathedral of the cave and in through the flaps of a fourth tent. This appeared to be an administrative area. There were banks of filing cabinets, a desk, several chairs and a tray with a kettle and jars of instant drinks.

"You want coffee?"

I shook my head and sat. She sat at the desk and pressed her hands between her knees.

"Nuna miyu was until recently a myth. But...," she gave her head a couple of shakes, like she was calculating time, "roughly eighteen months ago, maybe a little more, we found an original sample of nuna miyu. It was desiccated, hardened into a cup, but we were able to take small samples and analyze them, and what we found was a compound of certain fruits and leaves which formed a depressant hallucinogen so potent it would bring on a transcendent experience that would shatter the entire paradigm of reality for whoever ingested it."

"And they would assimilate whatever beliefs were fed to them."

She shrugged, then nodded. "Yes, in all probability."

"And now you have found this mixture and you want to weaponize it and sell it to the highest bidder."

"Harry!" She looked genuinely shocked. "I told you, Pasqüal is an altruist."

"You want to explain to me why an altruist is trying to learn the composition of a plant known to the Incas as soul poison?"

"Because despite the use the Incas gave it, the composition could be applied to a very wide range of uses."

"Like what?"

"Like curing chronic depression, for a start. Like curing paranoia and possibly even schizophrenia. Like curing Alzheimer's Disease—and many more. Harry, drugs are just chemicals, they are not good or bad. Those are artificial constructs invented by humans as a cohesive glue for society. Look at cannabis! Demonized for decades, and all the while it turned out it had an enormous range of beneficial uses. Well nuna miyu is the same!"

"Why should I believe you?"

"Why shouldn't you?"

She looked and sounded genuinely distressed. I said, "For a start, because you stole it from Dr. Calder."

She closed her eyes and buried her face in her hands.

TEN

"Pasqüal and I were going through a difficult time. I was in Boston staying with friends. It was September, which is the start of a particularly beautiful time in Massachusetts, as I am sure you know. My friends were both very busy people, he was head of the psychiatry department at the Harvard Medical School, and his wife was an extremely active social worker. So a lot of the time I was alone. That was fine by me because it gave me time to think and reflect on my relationship with Pasqüal. It was after a week or so I suppose, John—that was my friend—had a small dinner party. He was a very erudite, highly intelligent man, as you can imagine, and his interests were very broad. So, among the few guests he invited was Liz. We sat opposite each other at dinner and had a lot to talk about."

She smiled at the memory without meeting my eye.

"Like me, she was fascinated by Latin America, and we both shared a passion for the Inca civilization. She was of course far more knowledgeable than I was. I'm afraid we quite excluded the other guests from the conversation and spent the whole night completely absorbed in each other. I have sometimes wondered if John did not invite her deliberately, knowing that we would fascinate each other. Whatever the case may be, we agreed to meet the following day for lunch, and I told her about Pasqüal and the problems I was having with him."

Now she looked at me and paused.

"I know how Liz is with other people. She is brusque and abrasive, and rude. But she was not like that with me. She was gentle and kind, and very understanding."

She paused again, looking at the deep black mirror of the floor beneath her feet.

"In the end, after a couple of weeks, I returned to Geneva and to Pasqüal. We never discussed Boston. It was not necessary. Liz had helped me to know myself, we had spent a beautiful time together, but we had both known from the start that it could not last."

She took a deep breath and shrugged her shoulders. "Is it karma? Is it fate? Do we create our own future in our unconscious mind? Within the year the Pasqüal Pharmaceutical Company had made the arrangements for me to come here and research the plants in this valley, and quite independently Liz had come to start her dig."

"You didn't discus San Julian and Apusupay when you met in Boston?"

"I would be lying if I said we hadn't discussed it, along with a thousand other things we discussed, but we certainly didn't arrange to be conducting research in the same valley, in the same town, and at the same time. That would be absurd. Christ! The only reason we didn't wind up at the same hotel was because when I went to book Angie's was full. Otherwise we'd have been a couple of doors from each other!"

"Yeah, right, well I'm afraid my karma ran over my dogma and I just don't believe in that kind of coincidence. So you met here by pure chance, were utterly amazed, and took up where you left off in Boston."

Her face said she was less than amused.

"You can be a real cynical bastard, you know that, Harry?"

"No, I didn't know that, Amanda. I'll make a note of it in my self-awareness diary. Meanwhile, back on planet Earth, you and Liz took up where you left off in Boston, right or wrong?"

"Right! The difference was that here, Pasqüal, John, Sally, the university, our families...all of that was a million miles away. What few foreigners there were here, mainly our teams, were hip and cool and totally involved in their research and their own relationships. The effect was very disinhibiting."

"This was during your first visit here, over a year ago?"

"Yes, almost two years. We spent a lot of time together, and we got very involved in each other's work."

"And she told you about the cup."

She nodded.

"We inspected it together. She was fantastically excited. Iron was not known to the Incas. Had it somehow found its way here through trade? Was this some indication that they had discovered how to make iron? The implications were huge." She took a deep breath. "But what I was much more interested in was, here was what was obviously a ceremonial cup, at what was obviously an important ceremonial site on Apusupay, the mountain sacred to the Supay, with a dried, coagulated residue at the bottom. The chances were very high that this was the nuna miyu referred to by the Spanish authors."

"So while she was in the can, dreaming about a future as the leading archeologist of her day, with her dream partner, you were scraping away a sample so you could analyze it."

"I'm not proud of what I did."

"That's big of you. Why didn't you just ask her? Sounds like she would have given you whatever you asked for."

She didn't answer, but realization dawned. I nodded.

"Because it wouldn't have been for you. It would have been for Pasqüal. You were never really that interested in Liz Calder, were you? Your real interest, from the start, was nuna miyu, and you were with Liz because you knew the importance of this site and you knew there was a good chance you could find residue of that drug in ceremonial vessels, or in mummified remains. So you stuck with her, with Pasqüal's full knowledge. I'll bet it went further still than that. I'll bet it was Pasqüal's idea."

"God, you're a bastard. OK, if you're trying to make me feel like a whore you managed it. Yes, when I told him Liz was coming to Peru because she thought she had found the remains of the Apusupay temple, he asked me to come out too. I had told him long ago about the nuna miyu drug they were supposed to have fed to the sacrificial victims, and we had often discussed their possible medical application." She shrugged, avoiding my eye. "So it was natural that he would want me to come here, knowing the importance of the research, and the fact that Liz and I had been close."

"Natural..." I watched her while she watched the floor. "Your husband actively arranges for you to have an affair with somebody else, so you can gain a business advantage for him, and you think that is natural. What have you got in your veins, Amanda? Lubricant and wires? Because to the best of my knowledge anyone with red blood in their veins would find what you and Pasqüal have done sick, immoral and deeply unnatural."

Her voice became a little shrill. "This from the man who calmly announced to me earlier today that he had killed someone before lunch, and proceeded to sit and eat his own burger and mine."

"Self-defense, Amanda, and I am wondering now how far I have to go to find the person who sent that killer."

She shook her head, then shook it again, furiously. "No! No, nonono! Pasqüal would not do that! He might bend the rules, but only to secure a medicine he truly believes could help millions of people! He would never harm another human being for gain! Never!"

"What about you, Amanda? Would you harm another human being for gain?"

She went to speak but the words got stuck in her throat. I leaned forward with my elbows on my knees, staring her in the face. "For a start, Amanda, prostituting your wife is not bending the rules. And in my book, a man who will prostitute his wife to advance his business, will not balk at hiring a hit man to eliminate an obstacle. And last of all, what you—both of you—did to Liz Calder was exactly that, to harm another human being for gain. What you did to Danny..." I paused and she went very pale. "I'm still wondering about what you did to Danny. You already had your sample, so what did you need Danny for?"

She stared at me for a long moment, and there was horror in her eyes. At last she seemed to snap out of whatever was going on in her head and she blinked and said, "I think we're done here. This conversation has finished."

She went to stand but I didn't move.

"That would be a mistake, Amanda." I said it quietly and she slowly sat down again. "You ask the guy up in the woods how much of a mistake that might be."

She sagged slowly back, like somebody had let some of the air out of her. "You wouldn't."

I smiled. "It's my job."

"And you have the effrontery to judge me, and Pasqüal."

"I didn't judge you. I just gave you my opinion. Now tell me, why did you kill Danny? Danny?"

"I didn't kill Danny. I have never killed anybody."

"Why did you seduce him?"

"Liz had pretty much stopped talking to me after..."

"After she realized what you were."

She closed her eyes and went on. "I knew she had had tests done on the contents of the cup, but I didn't know what those tests were, or what the results were. So I asked Danny to find out."

"He told you they were carbon-14 tests and the cup was at least twelve thousand years old."

"Yes."

"So why'd you kill him?"

"I just told you I did not kill him!"

I nodded. "You tell a lot of people a lot of things. Most of them seem not to be true." I gestured around me. "What about this? Two years of field research. What are you making?"

I saw the muscles in her jaw bunch as she clamped her teeth shut.

"Earlier you listed a whole lot of cures you were going to develop. So which ones are they? Cancer? Chronic depression? Paranoia?"

I stood and looked down at her.

"What happens now, Dr. Epstein? A call to Geneva? Is that what happened with Danny? You called Pasqüal?"

"No."

"You told him the tests she'd done were nothing to do with the composition of the residue. They were only to do with the age. And he told you, in any case, it would be better if you had the residue instead of Liz, so there was no risk of it getting into other hands. And you asked Danny to do you that favor, promising him wonderful rewards in exchange."

She shook her head. "No, that's not true."

"But he said, no."

"No!" She screwed her eyes shut.

"Because he was a decent, honorable kid, he said no."

"No!"

"And you called Pasqüal and told him Danny refused to play ball."

Her voice was just a whisper. "No..."

"And Pasqüal sent a man from Cusco to kill him." I took a step toward her, took hold of her chin and made her look up at me. "What are you making, Amanda? Who are you making it for?"

"I can't tell you. Only Pasqüal knows those details."

"You're a doctor of biochemistry and you don't know what you're making? That's bullshit, Amanda. What are you making here?"

"We are assessing the potential uses..."

"For two years? You haven't identified fifteen unknown plants and seven new types of fruit. You have spent two years back-engineering nuna miyu."

She didn't answer. She just said, "What are you going to do?"

"I am going to find out what you plan to use it for."

"Don't do that."

"And who your husband is working with."

"Don't."

"You want to tell me why not?"

"You don't know what you're up against."

"Oh, really? I thought I was up against an altruist who only cared about curing cancer, depression and Alzheimer's."

"Harry, you don't know what you're getting into."

"Maybe you should have explained that to your friend in the Jeep this morning."

"That had nothing to do with me."

"But it had everything to do with your husband."

She covered her face with her hands again. "Look, I don't know who you are or who you represent, but this has to stop and you have to go away. Tell your superiors they have made a mistake. There has been a breakdown in communication." She dropped her hands and stared at me. "Didn't you say you came from Washington? Well go back there! Talk to the people in Washington! Tell them to talk to the Pasqüal Pharmaceutical Company. You are not supposed to be here! You are supposed to leave me alone to do my work!"

I gave it a moment, then answered her.

"Everything you have just said has proved two things to me. At first, until this afternoon, I thought maybe they had made a mistake. But now you have convinced me they haven't. And second, you said I had no idea who I was up against, but everything you have said proves that actually, it is you and the Pasqüal Pharmaceutical Company who have no idea who you are up against."

I pointed in the general direction of the labs. "I am going to find out what that stuff is intended for. You'd better pray it's not what I think it is. Because if it is, I am coming for you and for Pasqüal, and anyone else who is involved. I don't care if it's here, in Washington or in the White House. You'd better get your affairs in order, Amanda. Carl Allen was right. Ukupacha is opening its gates, and the Supay are coming." I held out my hand. "Give me the keys to your Jeep."

She frowned, confused and got to her feet, reaching in her pocket. "Why?"

"You get to ride home with your boys. I'm taking your truck."

She stepped forward and placed the keys in my hand.

"Harry, I don't know what the nuna miyu is used for. As far as I know it has not been synthesized yet. They have only just started working on that in Munich." There was a desperate helplessness in her face. "It is just a psychoactive relaxant, used in the right way under supervision..."

"Are you out of your mind, Amanda? A psychoactive drug that is being prepared for synthesizing and mass production after just two years? The European MEA and the FDA haven't even heard of it yet! It could take years for the Pasqüal Pharmaceutical Company to get approval for this drug."

Her face flushed, then turned a sickly gray. "But we have very powerful supporters, and there are other markets..."

"You mean corrupt Third World governments that will allow you to sell your drug there for an under the table fee? So thousands and thousands of people get to be your lab rats and take your untested drug, while you get to observe them and see how you need to tweak it before it is distributed in the United States and Europe?"

"God!" She flopped back into her chair. "You sound like one of those awful woke teenagers! Harry, the drug is safe! I have tested it! It is safe! Do you know how tough the clinical trials are in Europe and the United States now? And meanwhile thousands of people who could be benefiting from this amazing concoction are spiraling into catastrophic depression, stress-related illnesses, stroke, heart attacks—and all of it could be avoided if you would just butt out and accept what I am telling you!"

"You have tested it?"

"On myself and a number of volunteers, yes."

I stepped toward her and growled, "And one of those volunteers was Danny, wasn't it?"

Tears sprang into her eyes. "Yes! But I swear to you! It had nothing to do with his death!"

ELEVEN

By the time I got back to my room, having parked Dr. Epstein's Jeep out front, it was just after five PM. I pulled open the tall French windows and stood leaning on the cast-iron balcony, watching the square. There was an hour of sunlight left still, but the ancient streetlamps were already glowing with a limpid yellow light among the foliage of the trees.

I pulled a cold beer from the mini-fridge and when I got back to the balcony a Nissan truck was rolling into the square with the badge of the Cusco police emblazoned on its door. It pulled up in front of the hotel and a man in a neat, gray-green uniform climbed out of the back and entered the hotel. I wasn't surprised when a moment later there was a rap at the door.

I took a swig and said, "It's open!"

There was a moment's pause, then the door opened and the man in uniform stood framed in the doorway. When he spoke he had a strong accent and sounded both Bs in Baumb.

"You are Mr. Henry Baumb?"

"Yes. You've come to the right place. And you?"

"Teniente Coronel de la Policía Nacional, Quillabamba, Atahualpa Flores," he said in Spanish, then added, "May I come in?"

"Sure, sit down, may I offer you a beer?"

"No."

He closed the door, put his peaked hat under his arm and crossed to the chair I'd offered him at the desk. I sat at the table, with my beer beside me.

"What can I do for you, Colonel?"

He regarded me for a moment without humor. "You do not seem very surprise to have a police colonel calling at your door, Mr. Baumb."

"That's because I was expecting you, Colonel." He arched an eyebrow and I explained. "I am assuming that Mr. Pasqüal Bouc of Geneva has telephoned his friends in Lima and in Cusco and told them that Mr. Henry Baumb needs to be put on an airplane back to Washington at the earliest possible opportunity."

"I don't know who is Pasqüal Bouc, and maybe you should not be so quick to assume corruption in Peru. Mr. Baumb. I receive two calls making complain about you."

"Two? Do I get to know who made these complaints?"

He smiled. "Of course, two compatriots of yours, Dr. Elizabeth Calder and Dr. Amanda Epstein. These are two valuable expatriates here, Mr. Baumb, and we take their complains very seriously."

"And what are their complaints, exactly?"

"That you are interfering with their work, molesting their workers and spreading defamation about them. Is this true?"

I gave my head a small shake. "No, of course not."

"Then please, Mr. Baumb, will you tell me what you are doing in San Julian?"

I thought about lying, then decided it was pointless.

"I am here to find out what happened to Danny Cooper."

"Danny Cooper committed suicide. The official report was sent to his family."

"The official report makes it a fact, Colonel, but it doesn't make it the truth. I can assure you that Danny Cooper did not commit suicide."

"You are saying that the Peruvian authorities have lied? That is a very serious accusation."

"No. I'm not saying that. Perhaps they made a mistake, perhaps the investigating officer overlooked something. It happens in the best police forces. What I am saying is that the initial investigation overlooked a couple of important facts."

He frowned hard. "What facts?"

I held up my right thumb and tapped it with my left index finger.

"For a start, have you been to the top of the Apusupay, where he jumped?"

"No, I did not investigate this case."

"Well, I can tell you that in order to land where he is said to have landed, in the Urubamba River, he would have had to walk almost two kilometers down a very awkward slope to get to a point where he could jump and fall into the river. Why would he do that? It makes no sense. Park, and then walk a mile to make a jump he could have made fifty paces away, from the south face of the mountain?"

He shrugged and spread his hands in a gesture he had inherited all the way from the Mediterranean. "Who knows what goes on in the mind of a man who has decided to die?"

"I'll tell you what goes on, Colonel, despair, and the feeling you can't take it anymore and you need to end it—soon."

"What other supposed facts did they miss, Mr. Baumb?"

"He had just spoken, fifteen or twenty minutes earlier, to Dr. Calder and she had told him that she was going to share the credit for the dig, and some sensational finds they had made, with him and that his future career was secured as an eminent archaeologist. He gets that news, he is over the moon, he climbs in his truck and drives right to the top of a mountain, having decided to commit suicide, finds the most awkward path to a point almost a mile away, walks for maybe ten minutes to get there and jumps, when, as I said, he had a perfectly good jumping site fifty paces away."

He made a kind of "Pfah!" sound and looked away at the French windows.

"It is a little odd, yes, but all it tells me is that he was out of his mind with sorrow and pain, because Dr Epstein had rejected him." He gave his head a little sideways tilt. "Dr Epstein is a very attractive woman."

"I had noticed, Colonel. But however desirable she may be, that does not explain his last known movements. He spoke to Dr. Calder about a discovery they had made. She told him to go directly and speak to his father about arrangements to announce their findings. If he did so he was guaranteed a future as a leading archaeologist. He, happy and excited—according to Dr. Calder— went to get in a Jeep and drive to San Julian to phone Washington, but instead he went to the top of Apusupay, where he died."

He took a deep breath. "It is hard to explain, Mr. Baumb, but it is not enough to reverse the findings of the inquest, or open another investigation."

"Was there an autopsy?" He drew breath but I interrupted him. "Don't bother. I know there wasn't. Because if there had been they would have found high concentrations of an unknown psychoactive drug." I sat forward and pointed at him as I spoke. "And that is part of the reason he acted as he did. He did not drive to the top of the mountain, he was driven, and when he got there, I believe he broke free and ran, but was caught and then thrown."

"This is fiction! You are inventing!"

"Am I? Then perhaps you can tell me who the cream Jeep belongs to that is currently sitting at the top of Apusupay."

"What?" He scowled. "What is this now?"

"When I went to the top of Apusupay to inspect the place where he was supposed to have been killed, I was followed, after about fifteen minutes, by a man in a cream Jeep. He tried to shoot me. We fought, I got away, he lost his footing and fell from the very place Danny would have jumped from if he had committed suicide."

His face flushed and his dark skin darkened further.

"And you did not report this?"

"To be honest, I thought I had, Colonel. But having recently met Dr. Amanda Epstein, I have fallen insanely in love with her and half the time I don't know what I am doing."

His face said he did not think that was very amusing. "I should arrest you right now for murder."

"Maybe you should, but you'd be wasting your time and you know it. Pasqüal Bouc is not the only person around here who wields power, Colonel. If I were you I'd be very careful about getting in the middle of anything. Two people have been killed already; one of them was an innocent kid, the other was a hit man."

His hand went to the Sig on his belt. "Are you threatening me, Mr. Baumb?"

"Not at all. I am not stupid, Colonel. I am giving you some friendly advice. My sources tell me this is going to get a lot uglier before it's over."

"Your sources?"

I nodded. "By the way, who is Carlos Allende? Or Carl Allen?"

"This is your source?"

"I don't know. I just wondered if you knew him."

"This name is most common in Argentina or in Chile. Why do you ask about Carlos Allende?"

"I received an..." I allowed an ironic smile to slide up my cheek. "I received an anonymous letter from someone who signed the letter Carl Allen. I say anonymous because I believe the name was false. I believe it might have been Carlos Allende, or maybe something completely different."

"You should give all of this information to the police, Mr. Baumb."

"Yeah? Only according to you no crime has been committed."

"You have killed a man."

"No, he slipped and fell. I tried to call but, you know, there is just no signal up here, plus the lack of oxygen is playing havoc with my sense of time, and right now I was on my way down to Quillabamba to report it."

"Where is this letter?"

"Washington DC."

His eyes became cautious. "Washington DC?"

"Yes, Colonel, in an annex to the Capitol Building."

He stared at me for a moment, then drew breath and went to stand.

"I will require you to stop molesting Dr. Calder and Dr. Epstein. I also inform you that you have no jurisdiction in this country to conduct criminal investigations. My advice to you is to go home, Mr. Baumb. You are not welcome here. Next time we speak, I will not be so tolerant."

"Thanks for your advice." I jerked my head toward the door. "You know the way."

He gathered his tight-assed, strutting dignity about him, marched to the door and slammed out. I guess he figured the title of colonel entitled him to at least have doors opened for him.

I watched the darkness close in suddenly outside my bedroom window, and shortly afterwards Liz Calder's archeologists started to arrive in Jeeps and trucks. A couple of them dropped into chairs at tables and started ordering cold beers. Others went inside and I heard them talking and tramping as they made their way to their rooms. After a while I saw Karina Aalto emerge from the hotel onto the terrace and sit herself in a corner under an orange tree with a book. Five minutes after that a Land Rover rolled up and Dr. Liz Calder emerged from the passenger seat, looking scrubbed and clean, with fluffy hair. With her was a swarthy man in his fifties, with graying hair, a white shirt and gray, pleated pants. He got out from behind the wheel and they made their way to the terrace. They sat at a table and Liz's minions began pulling up chairs and joining tables. There was a lot of laughing and talking, and I notice the guy in the pleated pants was treated with a lot of respect.

I went down to the bar feeling suddenly mad. Cas was drying

glasses and looking unhappy. I leaned on the bar and said, "Give me a Scotch, will you? If you've got something better than Black Label that would be helpful."

She sighed and her shoulders sagged. After a second she put down the dishcloth and the glass and pulled out a bottle of Glenfiddich. She poured me a measure.

"I was going to ask you to move out tomorrow."

I knocked it back and put the glass down in front of her.

"Colonel Flores get to you? Fill it up and don't go away yet."

"No." She refilled the glass. "I told you when you arrived I don't want trouble, and the first thing you do is start causing trouble."

"Give me a couple of days and I'll be out of your hair for good." I raised the glass and paused. "Danny was killed, Cas. Don't you want to know who did it?"

She sighed again and wiped her dishcloth absently over the bar. "Not really."

I downed the second shot and pushed the glass across the counter. She eyed me a moment. "Are you going to get drunk?"

"Of course not. Did you ask about Carl Allen?"

"No."

"Jesus..." I said it without much feeling, then asked, "Who's the guy out front with pleated pants acting like he has something special with Calder?"

"Alfredo Quispe, the mayor."

"Of San Julian?"

"Of course. She entertains him a lot. So does Amanda, though she's more discreet about it. It helps with authorizations, permits, you know the kind of thing."

"Yeah, I know the kind of thing. So what does he get in return?"

She shrugged. I stared at her averted face while she polished, but my mind was absent. Amanda Epstein I could see offering favors, she didn't seem to have a problem with that. She seemed pretty liberated in that regard. But Calder? I didn't see her hopping into bed with anyone she wasn't pretty sweet on. That didn't jibe at all.

I took my drink and went and stood by the door. I wasn't immediately visible from the archeologists' table, where there were now about a dozen people gathered, and two waitresses delivering food and drink, but I had a direct line of sight to Karina Aalto, who was absorbed in her book with a glass of Coke in front of her.

She looked up as the waitress passed and called to her, and in that moment she caught my eye. We stared at each other for a long moment, while the waitress waited. Then she looked up and gave the girl her order. When the waitress left Karina's eyes returned to mine. I gave her a small nod. She didn't respond.

I went back to the bar and called the waitress who'd taken her order.

"Yes, señor?"

"When you take the blonde girl who's sitting alone her order, will you give her a message from me?"

"Of course, señor."

"Tell her that if she'll join me in here, I would like to invite her to dinner."

She smiled and disappeared into the kitchen. Cas was watching me, setting up some drinks on the bar. "You're such a romantic," she said, then did an imitation of my voice, "'Let me buy you dinner, do you mind if I grill you while we flirt?'"

"Fix me a steak and fries and quit griping. If my date stands me up we can flirt after the rush, and I promise not to grill you. I might roast you, stew you and even bake you. But no grilling tonight."

She slid the tray of drinks to the waitress and said, "Harry Baumb, you are one solid gold, genuine asshole."

Over her shoulder she shouted into the kitchen, "Un lomo con papas fritas!"

TWELVE

It was a long shot and it missed the mark. At a little after eleven thirty Karina Aalto entered the bar, crossed the floor to the stairs without acknowledging me, and presumably went up to her room. From the bar Cas leered at me and mimed holding her belly as she laughed. So I ordered another nightcap and she came and joined me to gloat for a bit.

"That's got to hurt," she said, straddling the chair next to me and filling two shot glasses.

"More than you know," I said truthfully and we knocked back the shots.

"One for the road." She poured again and spoke as she poured. "So, are you one of those guys who just walks up to women, 'Hi, how you doing?' and they fall into bed with you?"

I smiled and felt suddenly fond. Maybe it was the whisky, but I felt suddenly, more than usual, that life was a bitch, and she didn't deserve it to be.

"No," I said. "You won't believe me, but I am extremely shy. My work is my life, and I have never had a relationship that lasted more than a couple of weeks."

"Wow," she said. "Are you me?"

"No, you have a better figure."

"Ha!" She punched my arm. "No false modesty please, you know you look better than good."

"Is this the bit where we flirt and I don't grill you, but I can stew you if I want to?"

She snorted into her glass. "Another three-night stand?" She knocked back the contents and put the glass down on the table. "Nope. This is the bit where I clean up the bar and you go and wait for your very discrete date to show up."

I raised an eyebrow. "Is that what you think is happening?"

"C'mon!" she said, standing and gathering the bottle and the glasses. "Don't be naïve. Go get her, tiger!"

I sighed and stood. "Cas?"

"What? Don't you dare make a pass at me."

"I'm not going to make a pass at anyone tonight. I want to ask you about the mayor."

"What about him?"

"Does he live here in San Julian, or does he live in Cusco and come here once a year to meet the doctors?"

She blinked a couple of times. "You weren't kidding, were you? Your work is your life. You have an elf maiden from The Lord of the Rings waiting for you upstairs, and you're thinking about work."

"So where does he live?"

"He lives here in the village, Harry."

"Where?"

"The big house on the bend as you exit on the Quillabamba Road."

She went to turn but I asked her, "Has he always lived there? Family home? Did he inherit it?"

She stopped in her tracks and looked at me like I was crazy. "What?"

"Is it his family home? Did he inherit it? It's a simple question, Cas."

"No! He had it built after he became mayor. Anything else? You want his phone number?"

"No, no, that's fine. I'll see you in the morning."

I climbed the stairs, let myself into my room, stripped and stood under a cold shower for five minutes. Then drank a pint of water and prepared for bed. Outside my window the mayor's party was still going on, but with about half the people. As I pulled back the covers there was a soft but urgent tap at the door. I said, "Who is it?"

The tap came again, more urgent. I pulled on my pants and went to open the door.

"Well, I'll be damned!"

Cas had been right. Karina was looking behind her and at the stairs by turns.

"Please! Let me in quickly. Nobody can see me talking to you."

I stood back and she slipped in. As I closed the door she gripped my collar and stared into my face.

"Who are you?"

I put my finger to my lips and eased her toward the small lounge. There she sat on the edge of the sofa and I sat in a chair. She said again, "Who are you?"

"Did Liz send you to ask me that?"

Her blue eyes went wide and she shook her head vigorously.

"Liz must not know that I came here! Please, do not tell her!"

The fear looked genuine. "You know just about all I can tell you, Karina. I am a private investigator and I am here to find out what happened to Danny. Have you got something more to tell me?"

"But they can never know. They can never know that I have told you."

"You have my word. Told me what?"

"Danny, he was murdered!"

"How do you know that, Karina?"

"When the children were sacrificed to the gods, for a year they were fed on coca and maize beer, to make them peaceful and embrace Hananpacha and Viracocha."

"You told me that."

"Listen to me! But to appease Supay it was necessary to poison the soul so that Supay could eat that soul."

"You told me that too, Karina. How do you know Danny was murdered?"

"Because Danny told me that she was going to open the gates of Ukupacha. He had told her not to, and now they were going to kill him."

"He told you that? He told you they were going to kill him?"

"That is what Danny believed. She had discovered how to open the gates of Ukupacha, and she was going to allow all the Supay to come out and eat the souls of all people."

"OK, Karina, this is pretty much what you told me before. This is all superstition, there has to be something more concrete. There has to be proof somewhere. Right now it just sounds like Danny went crazy."

"He did go crazy. He went crazy and started to believe all of this crazy stuff about Ukupacha and the Supay. But, Harry!" She inched forward, reaching for my hands with hers. "Why did he go crazy?"

I remembered: "Because he was given..." but I trailed off because suddenly nothing fit.

She gripped my hands. "He was given nuna miyu! His soul was poisoned. He became obsessed. All he could think about was the gates of Ukupacha opening and the wraiths of the Supay rising up from the deep tunnels, filling the air and eating the brains and the souls of all whom they touched. On that last day we had lunch. Then, after, he went up the path to Apusupay. I never saw him again."

"You had lunch after he spoke to Dr. Calder?"

She thought about it for a second. "Yes, he came from talking to Dr. Calder, we sat together a while. He was so depressed, then he went to get the Jeep."

"You're sure he was depressed? He wasn't happy to start with?"

"No, no, he was so depressed."

"Was there anybody else there? Did anybody go with him?"

She hesitated. "Honestly, I am not sure."

"You think you saw somebody with him in the Jeep?"

"It's possible, but I am not sure."

I stood and went to the balcony. I could see Dr. Liz Calder sitting beside the mayor. There were four or five more people left at the table. They were all a bit drunk. Calder was not coming on to the mayor, and he was not coming on to her, but they were in very deep conversation. I turned back to Karina and sighed.

"Why did you take the name Carl Allen? And why did you tell me it wasn't you?"

"Danny was always talking about UFOs, Atlantis, government conspiracy of silence. He was crazy mad about all that stuff. One time he told me that his father and his father's best friend, Senator Randy Ortega, wanted to investigate an experiment that American government made with Einstein and other scientists. There was an informant in that case. He wrote a letter in many different inks, and he called himself Carl Allen. So Danny said to me, if ever he needed to write to his father for help, he could write as Carl Allen and his father would know. But when time came to write, it was too late for Danny. He was already gone. So I thought if I write in many colors, and sign Carl Allen, they will know it is serious. They will pay attention." She gestured at me. "Here you are."

"Yeah, here I am. But there is something you have to help me with, Karina. Opening the gates of Ukupacha is a metaphor. Ukupacha does not exist, and neither do the Supay. Danny may have been crazy in the end, but he wasn't in the beginning. So what did he mean when he said she was planning to open the gates to Ukupacha, and that the Supay were going to eat everyone's souls? That has to have a real interpretation."

She nodded. "Yes, I agree, and in the beginning Danny also said this. And when he became closer with Dr. Calder he said he was going to find out."

"Dr. Calder?"

"Yes. She was going to confide in him. But when she did..."

"He died."

"Yes." She spent a while looking at her hands, examining the backs of her fingers, like she felt there was something missing there. "He sometimes said, before he died, that he thought they were weaponizing something they had found."

"You keep referring to 'they' and 'them.' Who are 'they'?"

"This we never did find out. Dr. Calder has influential friends and connections in United States, but who they are we never discovered."

I sighed and sat down again. That didn't make much sense. Calder's influential friends in DC were Senator Ortega and Danny Cooper's dad. I had found Carl Allen, but after the big buildup, I found I was not much further on than I was before. If anything, I was more confused. I'd had some of my suspicions confirmed, but aside from that, I had learned little, except that Danny had indeed gone crazy and infected this impressionable young woman with his paranoia. I was going to sleep on it, but I was all but decided to call the brigadier and tell him it was a washout. There was a crime here, but no crime against humanity.

On an impulse I asked her, "Did Danny ever talk to you about Dr. Epstein?"

"I know he had a relationship with her, for a week or two." She smiled. "All the women wanted to be with Danny. He told me she was kind. She had a secret desire to win the Nobel Prize for medicine, and help stop suffering in the world. He said he did not trust her husband as such a good person. She thought he was, but Danny did not." She smiled a little more sadly. "I think he was jealous."

"Were you jealous?"

She laughed like I'd said something crazy, then covered her mouth, looking sidelong at the window. "No," she said. "Danny was very nice, I like him a lot, but he is not my kind of man. Too soft, too kind, too inexperienced. And too many women!" She laughed again, a very pretty laugh. "I need a very different kind of man."

I ignored the turn the conversation was taking and asked, "Karina, are you aware whether Dr. Calder and Dr. Epstein meet much?"

She shrugged. "Couple times Dr. Epstein come to the dig, before, in the beginning. Few times Dr. Calder goes to visit Dr. Epstein in her hotel. I think they were friends for a while."

"But not now."

"Not so much."

I turned it all over in my head, unable to make a decision. In the end I pulled Carl Allen's letter from my pocket and read the first paragraph aloud.

"Dear Senator Ortega, I am writing to you because I know yadda yadda... And I know that you have invested a lot of time and effort in making this excavation happen." I paused. "Danny told you that?"

"Yes."

I continued. "But you should know that some very bad things are happening here." I held up a finger. "Now, 'People are dying. People are being taken into slavery. People are having their souls sucked out and eaten.' What's that? People, in the plural, are dying. People are being taken into slavery? Who, where? People, again plural, are having their souls sucked out and eaten. Where is this happening, Karina? And to whom?"

"Everywhere."

I ignored her and went on. "There is awful evil at work here, Senator, yadda yadda... Now, here, 'Danny tried talking to the alcalde and to the police in Cusco, but they say he was crazy, and he has been warned to be quiet, or he will die, or worse.'"

I frowned at her. "Danny spoke to the mayor?"

She shook her head. "I did. But I did not want people from Washington, like you, going to the mayor asking about me. It could make me problems. So I say it was Danny. But the mayor told me I was depressed because of Danny's death. He told me if I wanted comfort I could go and visit him."

"You know an investigator would go to the mayor anyway? You were not hard to trace."

"I was in panic. I was very confused. I did not know what to do."

"And you went to the cops in Cusco?"

"They laughed at me and said I was crazy."

"You were lucky that's all they did. Who threatened you?"

"It was a phone call, to the hotel, asking for me. It told me to leave it alone, to stop talking and asking questions, or I would follow Danny, or worse."

"Man or a woman?"

"A man. American I think, but I am not sure."

"OK, but now I am going to ask you again, Karina, where are the slaves, the people who are being killed? So far as I can see, one person has died..."

"Two, if you count the man you killed."

"Yeah, then there's that."

"But most important, Harry, there are the ones you do not see."

"What are you talking about?"

"I am talking about the Peruvians. The invisible people nobody notices, who live in the tiny mountain villages. Danny Cooper dies and everybody notices. He has a father in Washington DC who can hire a private investigator to find out what happened to his son. But twenty-five, fifty, a hundred Peruvians die or disappear and nobody ever finds out. The police have instructions to ignore them. They cannot read or write, so they cannot protest. All they can do is accept."

I frowned at this sudden angle. "Are you telling me that the Indians in these valleys are being abducted and murdered?"

"I don't know if they are being abducted or murdered or something else. But Danny discovered that they were disappearing. In the beginning, when Dr. Calder first came here, the Indian communities in the mountains complained that she would be desecrating sacred sites. Shortly afterwards the most vocal protestors began to disappear. Danny liked to go and explore the villages and talk to the people, but soon he finds that they are avoiding him, some shouted at him and spit at him, and he wanted to know why. They told him why, not only was he desecrating sacred ground, but those who had protested were disappearing. Some said it was Dr. Calder who had woken the Supay. Others said it was men paid by Dr. Calder, or her university."

Now I saw it. Now it made sense. Icy spiders crawled through my skin.

"Karina, tomorrow I am going to take you to Cusco, and you are going to fly back to Finland. And you are never to talk about this incident, ever again. Do you understand?"

She nodded. "Yes, I understand, but I will not go. I will not let people intimidate me, Harry. That is why I wrote to the senator. We must be brave, and face evil, not run from it."

"Your life is at risk. They killed Danny. They tried to kill me."

"I am prepared."

"Jesus, Karina! This is not a..."

She stood and started to unbutton her blouse.

"Because I am at risk, Harry, I must sleep with you tonight. You will protect me."

I sat there, making like a goldfish, while she stepped into the shower.

THIRTEEN

At six AM she gathered her clothes and hurried down the passage back to her room. At ten past six she was back in my room, shaking me. Her face, already white, had turned a ghostly shade of pale.

"Harry."

I sat up, awake. "What?"

"They came for me last night. They came to kill me. Come, look!"

I pulled on my pants and followed her luminous form as she ran down the passage to her open door. I took her arm and pushed in ahead of her. The window was open and her duvet, along with the two cushions that lay under it, had been lacerated. I pointed at the cushions.

"You put them there?"

She nodded. "In case somebody is look in."

I thought fast. "OK, we are stuck with this now. Cas already suspected last night we were going to sleep together. Now this makes it obvious you were not in your room last night. This is going to bring a lot of heat down on you."

"I will continue to do my job."

"No."

Her blue eyes were defiant, her brows raised high, her chin thrust out.

"You forbid it?"

I snarled, "Yes. And we haven't time to argue."

"OK, so what do you suggest?"

Before I could suggest anything the door opened and Liz Calder pushed into the room. Her face managed to produce an expressionless scowl as she stared first at me and then at Karina.

"What's going on here?"

Karina's fingers went to her lips but she said nothing. I stared hard at Dr. Calder's eyes as they took in the details of the scene. Finally she looked at me again and I stepped toward her.

"Somebody tried to murder Charlie last night."

Her eyes narrowed and held mine. Her mouth curled into a bitter twist. "Fortunately for her you were interrogating her while it happened."

"I wasn't interrogating her, Liz, because as you knew all along, she doesn't know jack. But do you know what I have learned?"

"Amaze me."

"I've learned that people who get too close to you, wind up either dead or with hit men on their tails. Why is that, Liz?"

"Why don't you try and find out, Harry? You're living in Danny's fantasy!"

"Try be damned, I am going to gut every one of you and hang your heads from every church spire in Cusco, Quillabamba and San Julian. Hurt me and you'll pay dearly. Muss her hair, and I will dismember you alive and feed you to the ants."

"You're out of your mind. You don't know what you're talking about."

"Yeah, maybe you're right. But you know what? It doesn't change a damn thing."

She looked past me at Karina. "Charlie? You want to explain what this is all about?"

"I can't explain, Dr. Calder. I came in to get dressed and found the place like this."

"You know we have a confidentiality agreement, don't you?" Karina blinked at her a few times. Calder went on. "This man is an investigator. There are things you can't tell him."

I stepped up close to her. "Are you out of your mind? Somebody just tried to kill her!"

She thrust her face into mine. "And I'm sorry about that. But she still works for me and I have to protect my dig! And nothing is going to get in the way of that!"

Doors began to open down the hall and after a moment sleepy faces appeared, peering in. I growled, "Get out of here, and take your students with you."

When they'd all gone Cas was left leaning on the doorjamb staring at the bed.

"I knew you were trouble," she said. "The moment I saw you, I knew you were trouble."

"This trouble was here long before I arrived and you know it, Cas. This girl needs protection."

She shook her head. "Oh no, sorry. I am a single woman, living alone with a business to run. I haven't even got a weapon. How do you expect me to protect anyone, out here in the middle of the fucking Andes? We haven't even got a police station. The nearest cops are in Quillabamba, and you have to pay them to do anything more strenuous than answer the phone." She shook her head again. "Sorry." She paused, looking at the bed. "And I'm going to have to charge you for the bedding."

She left and I turned to Karina. "Get your stuff, bring it to my room. Your case, everything."

Half an hour later we were at breakfast in the bar, with Karina's bags stashed against the wall. I had my laptop on the table, plugged in to Cas's router. Cas was sitting with us, looking unhappy. Her tone had changed a little.

"I'm sorry," she said, and laid her hand on Karina's. "I am really. I'd like to help. But I'd be useless and we'd both wind up..."

She glanced at me like I should supply the ugly word. Instead I said, "Don't sweat it." To Karina I said, "I've booked you on a flight from Cusco this afternoon. You go via Lima to New York. I'll have someone meet you there and put you on the next flight to Finland."

Cas smiled at me. "So you are a good guy under all that bullshit."

I didn't return the smile. "I don't know if I'm a good guy, Cas. But you were right. There's no way Charlie can stay here, and there's no way you can protect her." I shrugged and smiled. "Who was going to protect you, right? Doesn't leave many options."

I closed the computer and stood. Karina drained her coffee. I looked down at Cas. This time I didn't smile.

"I'm taking Charlie to Cusco, to the airport, but I'll be back. And when I return, I am going to go hunting." I leaned on the table, looking into her face. "I am going to find out what's going on here. When I find out, I am going to start punishing people. It will be ugly, Cas. Even the Supay are going to cover their eyes and look away."

She tried to laugh, but it wouldn't come. Finally she said, "You're serious, aren't you."

"Yes, Cas. I am very serious." I picked up Karina's bags. Karina and Cas hugged, and then we walked out to the waiting Land Rover.

I pulled out of the main square and headed toward the Cusco Road, past a jumble of low, mismatched houses in pink and blue and yellow, with curtained doors and iron bars on the windows. Pretty soon the houses fell away and we followed the road for half a mile into the countryside until we came to a sharp, left-hand bend in the road. On the right there was a grass verge with a brick wall and an iron gate in it. Beyond the wall there were trees I could not identify, but they formed a dense, impenetrable wall.

I pulled up in front of the gate, climbed out and walked to the intercom on the wall. A woman's voice answered.

"Si, digame?"

In my faltering Spanish I said, "Soy Henry Baumb, quiero hablar por favor con el alcalde."

There was a long pause then. I had told her I wanted to talk to the mayor, and I figured she'd gone to get him. Eventually the gates buzzed and clicked and swung open. I climbed in the Land Rover and drove through, as they closed again behind me.

We were on an area of flatland among the peaks. It was at one extreme of the same plateau where San Julian had been constructed. The drive cut through it, direct to the house, with expanses of lawn and exotic trees to either side. There were banana trees, tall palms and araucarias, clustered into bizarre copses, with paths, small canals and fountains weaving between them. I figured it was the garden of a man who had just discovered he was rich.

The house was built on several levels, with towers, cones, domes, terraces and verandahs thrown together with the kind of glorious abandon you can only have when you are completely ignorant.

As I pulled up out front, two tough guys in cheap suits stepped through the door onto the porch. One of them had a ponytail all the way down to his ass. The other might have been his brother. There was a strong resemblance, only the guy with the short hair had a deep scar that pulled his mouth down into an ugly twist. He was the one who spoke as we climbed out.

"Vengan con nosotros."

We followed them up some steps to a verandah and in through the kind of heavy, iron-studded oak door favored by barons and dukes in medieval European castles. Beyond them was a terracotta-tiled entrance hall with a very white statue of Pachacutec holding up a banner. There were palms here and there and a tiled staircase that ascended to higher floors. The tiles had small blue flowers on them, which was kind of bizarre.

At the top of the stairs the landing made a dogleg on the right. We went down the short section toward the back of the house, where there was a window with a view of the town and the mountains rising around it. Here there was a single door. Ponytail hammered on it and a voice from inside said, "Vengan!"

He opened the door and we all went inside. The mayor was sitting behind a large desk made of deep, red-brown wood. He was in a black leather chair with his back to a panoramic window. The view was of the plateau, and the peak of Apusupay. He sat staring at us a moment without speaking. Ponytail was standing just behind Karina, and Ugly Scar was just behind me. The feeling wasn't friendly. The mayor's eyes moved over Karina then shifted to me.

"Mr. Baumb. You are lucky to find me in. I was about to go to my office in the Town Hall."

"Yeah, I figured it was before ten, you'd probably be at home."

His eyes narrowed a little. "What can I do for you and Charlie?" Before I could answer he turned to her and smiled the way a snake might smile at a field mouse right before lunch.

"I was talking to Elizabeth last night. Everyone was there but you were in the corner, alone, reading your books. You did not join us. Such a good girl, always studying, but sometimes you must relax."

"I had a lot of work to do, Mr. Quispe."

"Liz has a lot of hope with you, she told me she thinks you are a very promising archeologist. You can become an eminent, famous professor if you let us help you, Charlie."

I was getting kind of antsy so I cut in. "That's real nice, Alfredo, but I'm afraid we haven't much time, so I am going to cut to the chase." He looked at me like he might enjoy injecting poison into my eyeballs. Before he could answer I went on. "There is a potential problem. How many men have you at your disposal in your house?"

That surprised him. He frowned real hard, gestured at the two boys and said, "Two. Problem? What kind of..."

But by that time I had already turned to face the Ugly Scar, bent my left knee and driven my left fist deep into his liver. That is an instant KO.

When I turned to face his friend with the ponytail he was dodging past Karina to rush me, with astonished eyes and no clear idea of what he was going to do when he got me. I figured they didn't get a lot of violence up here. I stepped forward and drove a right straight lead into his jaw. That's also an instant KO. I pulled the P226 from under my arm, shot them both in the head and leveled it at the mayor's face. His jaw was slack and his eyes were wide.

"OK, Alfredo, I am going to give you every opportunity, and I strongly advise you to work with me. You understand?"

His mouth moved, his shoulders hunched and his hands spread. He looked at Karina but she was staring at me wide-eyed too. I snapped, "Hey! Alfredo! I'm here, look at me. Don't look at her, look at me. The clock is ticking and we are running out of time. I am going to ask you some questions. If you lie, I will hurt you. If you are vague, or evasive, I will hurt you. If you do anything but give me a clear, honest answer I will hurt you. Do you understand? Answer me."

"Yes, I understand, but what is going on? Charlie...?"

I cut him short. "You do business with Dr. Calder?"

"Yes, some..." He shrugged.

I went around the desk, grabbed him by his collar and dragged the chair over backward. He sprawled on the floor. I knelt on his chest, smacked him in the face and shoved the Sig into his thigh, right near his family jewels. I heard a small squeal from Karina but ignored it and snarled at the mayor.

"You get one more chance, Alfredo. I am not playing games here. I have killed a lot of men and I have no problem killing you. You have one chance to live, and come through this uninjured. You answer my questions clearly and precisely." I snapped at Karina, "Tell him in Spanish!"

She fumbled for a bit, then said, "Conteste claro y preciso, por favor."

"Next time you are vague or unclear, I will blow off your left kneecap. Do you understand me?"

"Yes, yes. I understand."

"What kind of business do you do with Dr. Calder?"

His lips had gone a pale pink color and there were beads of sweat on his forehead. He said, "I," four or five times, then, "I give her license to excavate, I talk to friends in Cusco, they have contacts in Lima, I make it easy for her." He could see by my face my patience was running low. "In exchange, she, she give me... special things she finds."

"What kind of special things?"

He tried to grin but his mouth was quivering too bad. "Artifacts, statues, stones..."

He trailed off because I had holstered my Sig and I was pulling a handkerchief from my pocket. I said to Karina, "If you don't want to see this, step outside."

With my left hand I stuffed the handkerchief in his mouth, with my right I pulled the Fairbairn and Sykes from my boot and drove it into his thigh. The scream was horrific, even through the handkerchief. His face bulged with the effort and the veins stood out in his neck.

I removed the handkerchief. His eyes were dilated and he was half unconscious. I looked around. Karina was still there, goggling.

"Snap out of it! I warned you. Go to the dresser. See if you can find some brandy."

She did, took a slug and brought it over to me. I dribbled some on his lips, then slapped his face a few times till he came round. When he had focused on me I held up his left hand.

"Next time, I take your finger. Get real, Alfredo. I am very serious. I need you to be serious too."

He didn't answer. He started to sob. I gave him a small slap and said, "Alfredo, nuna miyu. Tell me about it."

Now his eyes went wide. "No, no, how can you know?"

I lifted his hand and put the blade to the bottom joint of his baby finger, like I was going to peel an apple. He panicked and reached out his other hand, fending off the blade, blabbering, "No, no, no, I tell you! Please! I tell you! Please, no my finger!"

"Enough already! Talk!"

"She give us, she give me, she is proportion, providing..."

"What, goddamit?"

"Nuna miyu! She giving us nuna miyu!"

"What the hell for? You take the stuff?"

He swallowed, staring at me like I was crazy. He shook his head. "No, I don't take it. I cannot take it. It destroy your soul. We are giving it to the workers. The workers take it. They work real good."

I felt my skin go cold. A terrible stillness came over me. I could hear my heart pound in my chest. "The workers? What workers?"

"All my workers, on the farms, but especially in the mine. The gold mine in Madre de Dios. Is very hard work. Nuna miyu is good for them."

FOURTEEN

I DRAGGED HIM TO HIS FEET, PICKED UP HIS CHAIR AND threw him in it.

"Gold mines? What is he talking about?" I turned to Karina, who was still staring at me wide-eyed. "Ask him..."

But he interrupted me, "Mr. Baumb, I understand you. My English is good. I was in United States, also England and Europe. I speak English good."

I turned and stared at him. Bits of the puzzle made sense: the corners were there, the straight edges, the sky and the grass; but it was the bits in the middle, the farms, the gold mines, the tunnels and caves, and field labs and digs. None of that made any sense at all.

I pointed at him. "Listen, pal, I have been in palatial houses of people who were not rich enough to own gold mines. Your house is OK. It's in the Andes and you need a fucking helicopter to get here! My house is in Manhattan and it's bigger than yours, and I am not rich enough to own a gold mine!"

He went very quiet. Then he nodded. "It is not so simple."

I turned to Karina. "Take his shoelaces, tie them tight around his leg, above the wound."

She blinked a couple of times, then hurried to do what I'd said. To the mayor I said:

"So explain."

He watched Karina undo his shoelaces a moment. His skin was pasty and he was losing blood. He winced as she pulled the knot tight, then turned to me.

"Gold mining is controlled in Peru. It is almost impossible to obtain one license, but in Madre de Dios province there is a lot of illegal mining. Many mines open, and many bandidos who are protecting the mines, and stealing also the mines."

"Your mine is illegal?"

He nodded. "Also, the biggest customers to buying the gold are from USA. They say the risk for them is very great, if they are caught buying illegal gold. So," he made an ironic face, "the price they pay is not market price."

"So you aim to reduce your outgoings by not paying the workers."

"They are not suffering, we give food and water..."

"That's the last time you're going to justify what you're doing. Next time I blow your head off."

He swallowed and I went on. "Who's idea was this?"

He looked at the P226, then at my face and swallowed. Karina stood and backed away from him. He watched her and looked at me again. He held up his hands.

"Don't shoot me. I am telling the truth."

"Who's idea was it?"

"I don't know."

I raised the weapon and he held out both hands toward me, like he could ward off the burning lead with his hands. He was babbling as he did it, "No! No! I will lie if you want! Don't shoot me! What you want me to say?"

This was one of the two big problems with torture. Most of the time what the victim tells you is not reliable, because they will tell you anything to make you stop. The other was that it made me sick to my stomach, even when the victim was a piece of shit like this guy who deserved everything he got. I lowered the pistol.

"Don't lie," I said. "In the end it will be worse. Explain. What do you mean, you don't know whose idea it was? Was it yours or Dr. Calder's?"

His eyelids were sagging. His breathing was shallow and ragged. He was going into shock. I took the glass of brandy I'd dribbled on his lips earlier and put it in front of him.

"Whose idea?"

He picked up the glass with both hands and sipped it. Doctors will tell you spirits are no good for shock. I guess doctors don't often go into that kind of shock. Ask a special ops soldier. You'll get a different story. He pulled off half the glass and sighed.

"Dr. Calder is a very careful woman. Long time ago we talk. A little time after she first started to dig. We meet in Angie's. I remember she was dining with friends. She is seca..."

He was beginning to ramble, but I had no choice but to sit it out. I glanced at Karina. She shrugged and said, "Dry?"

He said, "Dry, dry woman, not friendly. Not simpática, but always with people all around. She is so intelligent. People want to chupar! Suck her intelligence." He closed his fists, mimicking somehow the action of sucking.

"Who was there?"

"Students," he looked at Karina, "she, Charlie, Amanda, they was friends then. She was with a friend."

"Wait, who was with a friend?"

He smiled. "Everybody was with friends. Liz with so many friends, Amanda with her friends, and everybody happy to see el alcalde!"

I looked at Karina. "This making sense to you?"

"Yes, maybe."

To Alfredo I said, "So what happened that night?"

"We talk. She and I, separate, we go away, apart, and start talking. Like many Peruanos, especially who live in the Andes, I am know a lot about Incas and Inca history." He gave a small laugh, staring at the edge of his desk, like he was talking to the desk instead of us. "She knows more than me! She knows so much!

"And we start to talk about difference..." He paused, raised an index finger and wagged it up and down. "Difference, between sacrifice to the gods, Viracocha, Pachamama..." He rolled his hand in a slow "on and on" motion. "The gods! And sacrifice to the demonios! Supay!" His head flopped back against the chair. His eyes were closing. "When you go to heaven, the gods get you with love and make you home. When good people die, before death, peace come to them. She tells me, 'Alfredo, Incas knew this, and when good children were send to heaven with Viracocha, they giving them coca and beer to make them feel good when Viracocha embrace them.'"

I pressed him, "So it was her idea?"

He shook his head and tried to focus on me. "No, listen, then she is telling me, when they make sacrifice to Supay, they give them no coca and beer, they are give them nuna miyu. But nuna miyu is no bad. Nuna miyu take away suffering. It protect the people from the Supay because when they come to eat your soul, you feel nothing. Nuna miyu take away all the pain. This was compassion of Inca priests."

He shook his head. "I tell her, 'Nuna miyu is myth. Is a legend from the Spanish. There are no evidences. All the mummies we find, they do the test on the hair, they find only coca and chicha, beer.' She laugh, and she tell me, 'This, Alfredo, is because sacrifice to Supay is only done in one place. Apu-supay, the sacred mountain of Supay. The one place, the only place, where can you find the ingredients of nuna miyu.' I tell her she is crazy."

"Liz said this? Liz told you it was the only place you could find the ingredients? Not Amanda?"

"No, Liz."

"So, what happened?"

"So one week after, I am receive a letter from Cusco. It is posted in Cusco. Address to El Alcalde de San Julian. When I am open the letter, inside I find black powder, and one note which is saying, 'Make tea and give it to one worker, make him work twenty-four hour, he will do what you want.'"

He stopped. After a moment I said, "And?"

"I give it to my maid. I am no marry. She clean every corner of the house till it is shining. Then I tell her, 'You come to the bed with me.' And she come, no problem."

"Dr. Calder sent you this powder?"

"I see her next evening in Angie's. I tell her, 'This powder you are send me is wonderful!' She tell me, 'I don't know what powder you are talk about.' I say, 'OK, but I want more. How can you give me more?' She laugh and tell me, 'Alfredo, you are already drunk?' But few days later one small packet comes and it have a lot of powder. 'You give this to all workers on your farm.'"

"And you did."

"I have a farm..." He gestured with his hand toward the window, like I'd be able to see the farm there. "Then, then I had one farm. I give my workers the powder." He gave a small, sleepy laugh. They like it. They want more. They feel nothing, no cold, no hot, no pain, no tired. Just they keep working, and they ask only for..."

He trailed off. I said, "Nuna miyu, poison for the soul."

"Yes."

"You know, Alfredo, there is a very special place in hell reserved for men who poison the souls of others. For..." I shook my head. "For beings like you, who steal human souls."

"Yes, I know. But soon I can buy another farm, and another. And only if I keep my farms high in the Andes, then there is no problem with the police. And all the time, by secret, my friend Liz is giving me more black powder for my workers. And soon, a man is coming to see me."

"What man?"

"He is from Europe, or maybe United States, I cannot tell. He is saying to me that if I will buy big piece of land in Madre de Dios, we can make gold mine. Much, much money. And to miners we can give black powder."

His eyes were closing and he was beginning to shiver with cold. I knew he was going into shock-induced sleep, so I slapped him hard across the face and thrust the brandy in front of him.

"You'll have plenty of chance to sleep when I call the doctor. Right now I have a couple more questions."

He grabbed the glass with trembling hands and took a swig.

"How do you get to the mine?"

"I have a small Cessna, it is only sixty miles nautical northwest. I fly myself. Is less than half an hour."

"And, does everyone at the mine take the nuna miyu?"

He gave a short laugh. "No! We must have guards there, to protect the mine. Four men are there, with guns. They are not my men. They are Liz's men, I think."

"What about the workers? How many of them are there?"

"Sixty, seventy, maybe more. Sometimes they die. Then we bring new ones."

"These are the men who disappear from the valleys and the mountains?"

"I don't do this. I just own the mine. The managers..." He shrugged.

"The managers. You mean the thugs with guns who run the mine."

He shrugged again.

I said, "OK, get the charts and the keys to the Cessna. We are going to the mine." Then I turned and looked at Karina, who was frowning at me. "What am I going to do with you?"

She narrowed her eyes. "You put a knife in his leg."

"Yeah. It's the kind of guy I am. Now what the hell am I going to do with you?"

"You think there are people who will kill me?"

I thought about it. "Yes. You talked to me. I came and made contact with you. You spent the night with me. Yes, yes they will want to kill you to stop you talking any more, and as an example to others who might want to talk."

"Then you cannot leave me alone. I cannot do those things

you do." She frowned and waved her fists, then said very seriously, "You are a very dangerous man."

Alfredo had pulled open a drawer and taken out some charts. He laid them on the desk and I saw there were tears on his face. "It hurts," he said simply. "It hurts a lot."

"Who's in the house, apart from these two?" I jerked my head at his two dead boys.

"Angelica, the cook, and Evy, the maid."

I turned to Karina. "Go find Evy, tell her we need the strongest painkiller she's got in the house. We'll be right behind you."

She left the room and I heard her feet running down the stairs. I dragged Alfredo to his feet and we hobbled across the floor.

When we got downstairs Karina was standing beside a maid in a black uniform with a white apron. She had black hair pulled back into a loose bun, and an expression of infinite sadness on her face. Karina was staring fixedly at her, but looked up as we came down the last flight of steps.

The maid held out a glass of water to Alfredo, and a small paper twist. He took the water, she opened the twist and spilled half a teaspoon of black powder into the water. Then she took a silver spoon from her apron and stirred the mixture until the water had become black.

Alfredo stared at it for a long moment, then he raised his eyes to stare at Evy. After a moment he shifted his stare to me. His lower lip quivered and tears spilled onto his cheeks.

"No puedo con el dolor," he said. He couldn't handle the pain, and he drained the glass.

Nothing happened. It wasn't like Daffy Duck or Bugs Bunny. There were no explosions in his ears and his eyes didn't bulge on stalks. He just handed back the glass and we hobbled out of the back door of the house.

There was a large, flat lawn. Beyond it, fifty yards from the house, there was a small hangar, and another twenty or thirty paces from the hangar was an airstrip of beaten earth.

We crossed the lawn and he did not complain. In the hangar we found a small desk and a couple of bentwood chairs. We sat him down and Karina helped me push the plane out of the hangar and onto the runway. The only change in Alfredo so far was that he had gone very quiet, and he looked real sad, like a man with a bad hangover. He was totally compliant and submissive when I led him to the Cessna and when I asked him, "How's the leg?"

He just said, "It does not hurt. There is no pain."

Five minutes later we were roaring down the runway and with a spring we were suddenly in the air, soaring north, with San Julian falling away beneath us. I banked right, east, following Alfredo's monotone instructions, and settled at twelve thousand feet mean sea level, which put me at roughly one or two thousand feet above the peaks below me, cruising at one hundred and forty miles per hour.

In the back, Karina, who had been almost as expressionless and passive as Alfredo, now lay down and curled up on the back seat, covered her face with her arms and began quietly to sob. I made a mental note to get her back to her family in Finland as soon as was humanly possible. Then I turned my mind to what I was going to do next.

After twenty minutes Alfredo pointed to a plateau above the convergence of two rivers that looked like a tuning fork. One of those two rivers flowed down from the plateau, like a gigantic C, and where it crossed the high flatland, I saw a huge, ugly, bronze gash in the land. It must have been a mile and a half long and six to seven hundred yards across. It was the gold mine.

"Call them," I said, "Tell them we're coming in."

FIFTEEN

He reached in his jacket pocket and pulled out his cell. I said:

"Wait. Tell them you're sending someone you want them to talk to. Tell them I'm a security consultant sent by head office. Tell them to be polite and helpful. Make it sound real."

He thumbed the screen and put the phone to his ear.

"Kay, good morning, is Alfredo. Listen, I am sending a guy to see you. I want you to be nice to him, OK? He come from Geneva. They sent him to look at security. Make him coffee, make him a tour, answer any questions. OK?" He listened for a while, staring out the windshield, then said, "OK. Call me when he gone."

He hung up and I said, "Go into settings and switch off your GPS." Over my shoulder I said, "Are you awake back there?"

"Yes."

"Then close your eyes and cover your ears."

I leaned across Alfredo, undid his safety belt, opened the door and gave him a hard shove. He watched me throughout, then fell easily into the void. There was no scream, no shout, just acceptance. The movement and velocity of the plane slammed the door closed, and then there was just silence. But after a few moments the sobbing started from the back again. I took off my jacket and handed it back to her.

"Get on the floor. Cover yourself. There should be a blanket back there too. Use whatever you can, but stay put and stay out of sight. I'll be gone ten minutes or so. Then I'll come back and get you out of here."

I came around in a wide arc and approached the airfield so the plane would be as far from the office buildings as was possible. I came in low from the east, overflew a cluster of huts and long, low wooden structures that had the look of a barracks, and hit the dirt runway beside the river. I slowed, taxied to the end and turned to face the way I'd come in. So anyone looking at the plane would see just the prop and the sun shining on the windshield.

I swung down and slammed the door and for a moment had the bizarre sensation of being on an alien planet. Rising sharply all around me, densely forested, narrow peaks towered, blocking out the sky, making the small plateau feel almost like some kind of amphitheater of the gods.

Except that where the ground should have been flat, green turf on the banks of the river, it had all been torn up in great gashes, rising in brutal strips up the sides of the slopes at the northern end. As I stood and watched, I could make out people, like small, slow black insects, laboring in the dirt and on the hillsides, where the trees had been ripped out to afford access to the earth. This was open cast mining. The labor was manual and for every four people I saw, one was a man or a boy, the other three were women and girls.

I started to walk along the short, beaten earth runway toward the dark green wooden buildings at the end. There, three large men in camouflage had emerged from a hut and were walking toward me.

As we drew closer I saw that the man in the middle was about six-two and in his late thirties. He had a crew cut, a fair moustache and powerful arms and shoulders. The man on his right was shorter, maybe five-eleven, about the same age, bald and clean shaven, with a radio jaw and very pale, psychotic blue eyes.

The guy on the left was younger, probably in his late twenties, athletic, with inch-short blond hair and cruel eyes that might have been green. All three of them carried sidearms.

As they stopped in front of me, the guy in the middle gave me a languid salute and tried to smile. His accent when he spoke was South African.

"How's it goin'? I'm Kay. I'm in charge of this shithole. These are Ken," he gestured to the bald guy, "and Stewart. They help me to keep things running smooth. Offer you some coffee, or a cold beer?"

I nodded. "Yeah, that'd be good. I'm Harry Bauer," I said, because I believe, where possible, people should know who killed them.

We turned and started toward the wooden structures. Kay asked me, "So, what is it we can do for you, Harry? The boss said we were to help you out where we could."

I took a deep breath, calculating the steps and how long it would take to get inside.

"I'm mainly interested in three things. The first is how the workers are performing in terms of obedience as against exhaustion."

He nodded a lot. "Oh, yeah. It's amazing. Never seen anything like it. They're like those fuckin' bunnies on TV. They just keep going, on and on and on. And not a fuckin' peep out of them." He laughed a sudden, harsh laugh. "Ken couldn't believe it, so the other day, the crazy bastard—" Here Ken, the bald guy with the pale eyes, began to laugh too. "He goes out, he picks a kid, must have been no more than eight or nine years old, she's loading rocks into a basket, and right in front of, must have been a hundred people, he takes out his piece and shoots this girl in the head." Kay stopped dead and turned to face me, placing the knuckle of his forefinger on my chest. "Can you believe, Harry, the rest of them did not even look up from their work!

They did not-even-look-up! Fuck, man! Placid does not come close to describing how these people are. And they just keep going."

I nodded once, turned and continued toward what I assumed was the office. They followed me in. As the door closed I asked, "What about the villages? Don't they send people out to look for them?"

Stewart, the young guy, answered. He was also South African. "Nah, they know what's waiting for them if they come anywhere near the mines. They either get shot or put to work."

Kay slapped the back of his hand against Ken's chest. "Get the man a beer, Ken. Get me one while you're at it." To me he said, "What else?"

"The powder. How are you administering it?"

He frowned, alerted. He had not liked the question. "Exactly as Alfredo told us to."

I took a bottle of beer from Ken and watched Kay's face a moment. Then laughed. "Nobody is questioning the quality of your work, Kay. On the contrary. It's just that we would rather get it straight from the horse's mouth, than from the mouth of the Peruvian mayor of San Julian. You guys are on the ground doing the work. Alfredo is in his house screwing the help. We'd like to hear it from you." I looked at them each in turn. "And I don't need to tell you gentlemen that cooperation and loyalty can quickly turn into promotion in Geneva."

They all glanced at each other and there was the trace of a smile exchanged.

Kay spoke. "We increased the dose. The air is very thin up here and they were dropping like flies, with exhaustion. So we sprinkled an extra tablespoon full of the stuff into their gruel once a day. And the boys'll tell you, performance improved overnight. They'll keep going now till they drop dead. Either they don't feel pain, or they don't know they're feeling it. You can hit them, kick them, whip them, they just keep going. I've never seen anything like it."

Ken put in, "Tell you, you could line 'em up and use 'em for target practice. They wouldn't run. They'd just stand there."

Stewart laughed. "We should do that one day."

I cut in. "Where do you keep the powder?"

Again the frown. He pointed out of the window. "In the shed. We keep it dry and cool, according to Alfredo's instructions."

I took a long pull on the bottle and smacked my lips.

"Alfredo deliver it himself?"

He nodded his head, and I could see he was becoming cautious.

"Yeah, mate. He drops it off once a month."

"You call them all in to eat..."

"Yeah, they all line up and they get a bowl of high-protein food, mostly rats and cockroaches..."

They all looked at each other and laughed again. I smiled. "I've had worse."

The laughter faded. "Right, and they get three tablespoonfuls of the powder sprinkled into the food."

"So, aside from the workers, there's you three guys and a cook? You're not worried about people moving in on you?"

"We've got two grunts cooking the grub. They're handy with an AK47. We're pretty well armed and Alfredo stays informed. I don't think there's any real risk." He made a kind of a wince out of the window, like he wasn't quite satisfied with the view. "You know what? Alfredo said to cooperate and give you any help you needed. But, I can't really see where these questions are going. I think I'm going to call him..."

I smiled and shook my head.

"That's really not necessary. He's dead. I threw him out of the Cessna before landing."

Kay had spoken to him only minutes before. They were struggling to make sense of what I'd just told them, and that gave me three full seconds to do whatever I liked. What I liked was to smash a hard left hook into Kay's liver at close quarters, while simultaneously pulling the Sig from under my arm. I put the cannon in Ken's face and said, "No."

Traumatic impact to the liver is devastating. It can rupture the organ and lead to death. Kay was lying on the floor with his eyes rolled back, frothing at the mouth and groaning. I put him out of his misery with a single shot to the head. Then I asked Stewart: "Where does Alfredo get the powder? Two wrong answers and I start killing people."

His hands were up, his green eyes looked scared and his mouth was having trouble forming words.

"Nah," he said, "nah, no, we don't know. We're not privy to that kind of information. We were just told to keep an eye on the workers and protect the mine."

I shot him through the middle of the forehead and turned to Ken. His pale blue eyes looked terrified. He was bordering on panic. "You want to give it a try, Ken?"

"For Christ's sake! He was telling the truth! They never shared that kind..."

He stopped suddenly because I had shot him through the head too. I told them both, "Wrong answer," and stepped over their astonished, motionless bodies and out through the door. There was a long hut about twenty paces away. The doors were open and I could see movement inside. I poked my head in and smiled. It was a kitchen, and there were two grunts making what looked like a stew. One of the guys was fat and had long blond hair and a beard. The other was skinny, with a dark crew cut. They had the radio on and turned it down as I smiled.

"Hi there. Kay is just showing me how things work round here, for the boss back in Geneva. You want to show me how you call the workers for their meals?"

The guy with the gut glanced at his watch.

"Well, it's a bit early. But there are loudspeakers on—" He inched toward the door, peering out through the window and pointing. "If you look, on the top of the posts, you can see them, like loudhailers. So when it's lunchtime we press that button over yonder by the door, on the intercom, and speak into the hand-piece. They hear it all over the mine."

"Cool, that's good. And they just obey and come right on in to eat."

"Like little lambs."

I came further inside and looked around, shaking my head.

"You know what I keep thinking? You guys must get a bit crazy. You must need regular 'R-and-R,' right? You could go a little nuts up here alone all the time."

The fat one laughed. "You ain't kidding. Once a week we take a truck and three of us follow the track down beside the river, and we let off steam down at Casa Gata, in Entre Rios. It's pretty good."

"Yeah?" I smiled. "I'll have to try it out. So how many trucks you got here?"

"Let me think, uh..." He turned to the thin guy with the dark crew cut and they stared at each other for a moment, calculating. I got bored as they drew breath to speak, decided it didn't matter all that much, and shot them both where they stood.

After a brief search I found the sack. It weighed about fifty pounds. I carried it to the bank of chemical johns they had beside the kitchen and dumped about ten pounds into each one.

Finally I went back to the kitchen and summoned the workers in broken Spanish to come to the yard in front of the offices. Then I called the brigadier.

"Harry."

"This is too complicated and too weird to explain over the telephone. I'm going to send you my coordinates. You need to send some specialists here. There are about a hundred men, women and children who have been drugged and used as slaves in a gold mine in Madre de Dios. They need to be collected, taken to a safe place and treated."

"Ah, there was something to the story, then."

"Yeah, there was something to the story. This same thing is being done on cattle farms in the region too."

"Have you finished?"

"Not by a long shot. There are powerful interests at work here, sir, so you had better be careful who you talk to."

"Don't worry about that. Just send me your location and I'll get some people there."

"OK, I'll call you from the air in a while."

I sent him my coordinates and made my way back toward the airfield as the workers began to drift in, in ones and twos from the mines, like extras from a bad zombie movie. Only what made these people shuffle and drag their feet was that their souls had been poisoned and their very will to exist had been sapped from them. If all we truly have is our minds—our spirits—then the theft that had been perpetrated upon these people was a crime heinous beyond measure.

As they drifted past me I pointed toward the huts, shouting in broken Spanish, "Vayan allí! Esperen. Hombres vendrán a ayudarles! Esperen allí!"

They should go and wait, and men would come to help them. I prayed I was not telling them yet another lie.

As I clambered into the small plane, through the windshield I could see the people beginning to accumulate in twos and threes. Some were standing, others were sitting on the ground. Some were going into the buildings, seeking who knew what. I wondered for a moment who the brigadier would contact; would it be people in the Peruvian government? Would they play it by the book? If so, I wondered what these people's lives were worth. Would they recover? Was there a cure? How do you cure a poisoned soul?

But that was beyond my brief and beyond my control. I looked in back. Karina was sitting up, staring at me. She had stopped crying. I slammed the door and started the engine, and she clambered up front, beside me. I gunned the engine and started the run down the airstrip.

We lurched into the air and the mine and the forest dropped away beneath us. As I banked right she asked me, "What did you do? What did you do back there? I heard you. You told those people to stop working."

I studied her face a moment, then looked ahead, out of the windshield, at the ocean of green canopy.

"You're asking, but are you sure you want to know?"

"Yes."

"There was information I needed. I got it from the guards who ran the mine. When I had the information I killed them."

"Why?"

I was surprised and showed her a face that said so. "Why? Because these bastards use a drug to destroy these peoples' minds, so that they will be pliable and obedient; so that they will be slaves, not only in body but in their minds and spirits too."

"Nuna miyu."

"Yes. I figure we don't need people like that in this world."

"But, who are you to decide that, Harry?"

I shook my head. "That's the wrong question, Karina. And it's part of everything that has gone wrong in this world. For every individual who abdicates responsibility, these bastards grow a little bit stronger and a little more numerous. The question, the real question, is, who am I not to decide that?"

SIXTEEN

We flew back to the mayor's house. There I made use of the computer in his office and bought Karina a passage from Cusco to Helsinki, printed her tickets and her boarding passes and made sure she was provided for financially for the journey.

"When you get there, you forget any of this ever happened. You never tell anybody about what you experienced here. I'm going to make sure nobody goes after you. OK?"

She had nodded quietly, with her huge blue eyes watching me. Then I told the cook and the maid that el alcalde had stayed at the mine and would not be returning for a few days; that until then they should take the time off on full pay. I told the maid to get me the keys to the mayor's Mercedes and, when they'd gone, I gave them to Karina.

"You drive this to Cusco airport. You park it in the airport parking lot. Touch nothing but the steering wheel, the gear shift and the door handle. You touch anything else and you immediately wipe your prints off with a handkerchief. When you get to the airport parking lot you wipe the wheel, the gear shift and the handle, and anything else you might have touched. Is that clear?"

"I take the car first to a carwash."

"OK, that's good."

"And you?"

"I have to finish what I came here to do."

"Kill more people?"

"You'd better get going."

"My things?"

"I'll have them sent to your parents."

I walked her out to the garage, watched her climb in and drive, with no show of emotion, as far as the gate. Then I watched the doors roll back and the car disappear south, toward Quillabamba and Cusco. When the gate had closed again, I went back inside and climbed the stairs back to the mayor's office, where his two goons still lay dead on the floor, with the blood beginning to crust around their heads.

I paused a moment to consider them. They had not committed crimes against humanity. But they had facilitated them, and attempted to protect those who had perpetrated them. I set the thoughts to one side and began a methodical search of his files, drawers and documents, sending photographs back to Cobra wherever I thought it was relevant.

"What I was looking for was some kind of demonstrable link between the mayor and Liz Calder, or the mayor and Amanda Epstein. After two hours of solid graft, I hadn't found one. Not anything you could call forensic proof.

But I had found something. It was a large document which I folded into a large manila envelope and took with me.

I went down, got in my truck and returned to San Julian. But I didn't stop at Angie's. I made the circus and turned down Calle Atahualpa Yupanqui, then took the first on the right and pulled up outside the Pachacutec Inca Hotel. The building looked 19th century trying to echo 16th century, with a heavy stone frame around huge wooden doors. Large windows behind iron bars flanked the doors on either side, and small, wrought-iron balconies jutted from the second floor. The whole building was a kind of adobe yellow, painted sage green up to a height of four feet from the road. The doorstep was gray granite polished to a high gloss, so it looked like marble.

I stepped over it and through a kind of porch with a wrought-iron door, and found myself in an internal patio with lots of plants in pots, a mosaic floor and a classical fountain in the middle.

Reception was beyond the fountain, where a thin man with a shiny bald head, very white skin and a nose you could open a can with, watched me approach. He tried to smile but obviously didn't know how, because all he did was show me crooked teeth under sad, amber eyes.

"Monsieur..." he said.

I leaned on his desk. "Can you tell me if Dr. Amanda Epstein is in? I have an appointment to meet her."

He picked up an ancient Bakelite telephone, dialed a number, tipped his head forward and rolled his eyes to look up at the ceiling in a way that should have been impossible. He held the pose for a long time, then suddenly dissolved into an infatuated grin. "Ah, Mademoiselle Epstein, ah!" He gurgled bashfully. "Pardon! Pardon! Madam! You 'ave a gentleman 'ere who 'as an appointment wiz you, a Monsieur...?" He made a question with his face and showed it to me.

"Baumb."

"Baumb."

"Tell her I'll meet her in the bar."

"Monsieur will meet you in the bar, madam! Merci! Merci!" He hung up and sighed with happiness, then directed a face of infinite sadness at me. "Such an elegant lady, in this terrible place. Mademoiselle Epstein will meet you in the bar in a few moments, Monsieur Baumb."

"Thank you...?"

He showed me his teeth again, the ragged survivors of a holocaust of alcohol, nicotine and sugar. "François."

I gave him ten bucks and he gazed at it like it was a photograph of Paris in the '30s.

The bar was on the left through a door framed by trestles festooned with flowering creepers. Inside, the walls were white, hung with occasional canvasses that were either Impressionist or abstract. The Impressionist ones were derivative but well executed and nice to look at. The abstracts were just cheats by some guy who couldn't draw.

I ordered a dry martini and found a table beside some French doors onto an internal patio paved with heavy, irregular stones. Low troughs held a variety of cacti, while terracotta flowerpots held hundreds of geraniums.

In less than five minutes Dr. Amanda Epstein appeared walking fast and with no expression on her face. She stopped at my table and looked down at me.

"I am very busy, what do you want, Harry? I haven't time to stop."

"Have a martini with me."

"I have just told you..."

"I heard what you told me. Sit down and have a martini." I glanced across the bar and saw the barman approaching. I saved him time. I showed him my glass, pointed at it and made the V sign for "two." He nodded and went back behind the bar.

Epstein said quietly and deliberately, "I haven't the time."

"Make time, Amanda. We need to talk. I have just come from Alfredo's gold mine."

She remained completely immobile for a full thirty seconds, then very slowly sat opposite me.

"You need to know," I said, "but you don't know how to ask without implicating yourself." I waited but she still didn't say anything. "Go ahead and ask, Amanda. You are already implicated up to your pretty blue eyes."

"That's not true."

"Why? Because you had Liz cover for you? Get real."

"That is not true."

"Have you ever been?" She gave her head a small shake. "You should. It's an education. You really get to see the true quality of humanity in the raw. There were a hundred people or more working the open cast mine. Three quarters of them were women and children. I saw little girls and boys out there who were maybe seven or eight years old. They were slaves, watched over by South African mercenaries with guns." I sat forward. "But that wasn't the worst thing." Her brows contracted over her eyes, where I could see real fear. "Do you fully comprehend what I have just said to you, Amanda? That the fact that women and children as young as seven or eight are being enslaved in a mine by men with guns, is not the worst of it. Do you understand that?"

"You know I don't."

"I'll tell you more. The women are systematically raped, and one of the children was shot in the head the other day, just to see how the others would react. But, Amanda, that is not the worst of it."

"I don't know what you're talking about."

"I am talking about men and women and children, whose only crime in this world is to have been born in the Andes near Apusupay, having their very souls robbed from their bodies and murdered!"

I saw the barman glance over at me and sat back in my chair, forcing myself to smile at her. I drained my glass and placed it on the table as he set down our drinks.

"So how's work, Amanda? Are you making much progress in your research?"

The barman took the empty glass and left.

There were tears in her eyes. She shook her head rapidly. "What you are telling me has nothing to do with me."

"Really? Oh, good. Say, I went to see the mayor just a while back, and we had a chat. He told me that he'd had several long talks with Dr. Elizabeth Calder, who told him that she had discovered the secret of nuna miyu, and that in exchange for a regular supply of that drug, which he would test on his various employees, including his maid and his miners, he would ensure that she had no problems getting all the grants and licenses that she needed. That courtesy seems to have been extended to you too, and the Pasqüal Pharmaceutical Company of Munich. Which is interesting because he also happened to let slip the fact that 'head office,' whatever that is, is located in Geneva. You still want to tell me it has nothing to do with you?"

"I swear I know nothing..."

"Can it, Amanda. For a start there is no way that Dr. Calder has the means, or the time, to produce that stuff in the quantities needed to run a mine. In the second place she hadn't the means to analyze the residue to find the formula. She needed your help to do that. You yourself told me you had taken a sample and done just that, and that Pasqüal Pharmaceuticals was actively studying how to manufacture it."

She was still shaking her head, like she'd got stuck. "I swear, Harry. I swear I had no idea."

I laughed out loud. "Are you seriously telling me that Dr. Elizabeth Calder and your husband are in league, and have cut you out? Seriously?"

"I don't know. I don't know what's happening. I swear, Harry, I have no idea. But I had nothing to do with that mine."

"Nothing?"

"Nothing, I swear!"

"Then how come you own a one-fifth share of it?"

She closed her eyes and sank back in her chair. After a moment she said: "Not Entre Rios, in Madre de Dios?"

"That's the nearest town, yes. You didn't know you owned a gold mine there?"

She opened her eyes and covered her face with her hands. "Of course I knew."

I sat back and watched her a moment.

"I think it's time for a reality check, Amanda. I think you and reality have a special kind of relationship. A bit like you and men. Nice to hook up sometimes, but don't encroach too much on my freedom."

"Please stop that."

"No, I think I'll keep right on going. Here's today's serving of actual, real reality. You know Karina, AKA Charlie?"

"Yes, I've seen her around."

"OK, well last night they used her to try and kill me, to silence me. So today I took her with me to the mayor's house. There I killed his two guards and stabbed him in the leg to make him talk. Then I took him and Karina out in his Cessna 170, to the mine—your mine. When I had the mine in view I threw him and Karina out of the plane."

Her eyes were growing wider and wider with horror. I pressed on.

"Before I threw Alfredo out I made him tell the supervisor I was on my way, that I'd been sent from head office—that would be head office in Geneva, Amanda—and to cooperate with me. So, when I'd got all the information I needed from them, I killed them too. That's quite a morning's work: seven people in just a few hours." I gave her a moment, then went on. "You would be very wise, Amanda, to cooperate with me. I need someone who can put the finger on the big boys in DC, Munich and Geneva. Everybody else dies. Are you assimilating this reality, Amanda? Nobody can make this go away. You have to face this and deal with it."

She took a paper napkin from the table and dabbed her eyes.

"You seem to think I am some kind of psychotic child who is out of touch with reality. I assure you, Harry, that that is not the case. I am fully aware of the horror of what you are telling me, and of the kind of monster you are. But however much I face it and deal with it, and however much you threaten me, I cannot tell you anything about the mine because I don't know anything about the mine!"

I sipped my drink and as I set it down I said, "Sip. I don't want to attract attention. So, if what you are telling me is true, that puts you in a very bad situation. Because neither I, nor my superiors, are going to believe that you could be so intimately involved in something you knew nothing about; but at the same time you will be of absolutely no use to us."

"So you will murder me?"

"Execute."

Her eyes blazed. "Now it is you who are out of touch with reality! Execution without a legitimate trial is murder!"

"You own a mine jointly with Dr. Liz Calder, Alfredo the mayor, Pasqüal Bouc and the Pasqüal Pharmaceutical Company of Munich. How can you claim not to be involved?"

She made the face of despair and threw her hands in the air. "It was during his visit here, when I told him about Liz's discovery. He was very interested and we invited Alfredo to dine with us. Honestly I found their conversation boring and I'm afraid I spent too much time flirting with Danny Cooper, trying to make my husband jealous. Naturally it didn't work. The next day he told me he had made an agreement with Liz and Alfredo to buy a large chunk of land in Madre de Dios. It was cheap because it was very inaccessible and very close to a national park, so very difficult to develop. He is always doing things like that, so I said fine. When the time came I went along and signed the documents before a notary, and some time after that he told me they had decided to try mining gold there. Naturally he was full of how they were going to do it in a way that ensured the miners benefited fully."

She paused and I tried to read her face. She looked sincere. "Harry, I swear to you that if Pasqüal had had the slightest idea of what was going on he would have come down on Alfredo like a ton of bricks."

I nodded a while. "So the drug which is being tested on the miners does not come from the huge, multinational pharmaceutical company that owns the mine. It is being supplied by the archeologist who spends eighteen hours a day, seven days a week at her dig."

She frowned. "No, of course not!"

I leaned forward, feeling the anger rising inside me. "There are five owners of that mine, Amanda!" I held up five fingers. "One of them is a pharmacologist, two others are owners of that pharmaceutical company. All three of them were active in stealing and developing the formula for that drug. Now you tell me, who is supplying that drug to the mine?"

She closed her eyes again. "I don't know!"

"Boy, you had better wise up, sister. Because things are not looking good for you."

Her face began to dissolve. Her voice was barely a whisper. "Are you seriously threatening to kill me?"

"Somebody stole a sample of the nuna miyu that Dr. Calder found. We know that was you because you admitted it to me at your lab. Somebody analyzed that sample and sent it to be studied by Pasqüal Pharmaceuticals so it could be synthesized. We know that was you because you told me so. We know that while the Pasqüal Pharmaceutical Company of Munich was working on that process, you remained here to study and identify the plants and the fruits that go into that drug. I know that because you told me. So explain to me, show me, convince me: how are you, your husband and your company not the person supplying the mine with that drug?"

She shrugged and wiped her cheek.

"I don't know, Harry. I can assure you that if I had set this up, it would have been arranged a lot better, and as soon as you arrived I would have had every angle covered. But I am not a criminal, and I did not do this. Perhaps Liz leaked it to somebody. Perhaps Danny leaked it to somebody. He was not exactly smart or discreet. I mean, for God's sake! You don't need a lab to process the stuff! The Incas did it right here. All you need is to know how. Liz is not your woman because she is good and decent and honorable, but somebody close to her could be."

I sat with my drink halfway to my mouth, watching her and listening to her, and thinking, in spite of myself, that what she was saying made some kind of sense.

Somebody close to Dr. Liz Calder.

SEVENTEEN

I SAT A LONG WHILE IN SILENCE, WITH DR. AMANDA Epstein watching me. Eventually she said, "Harry, I'm sorry, this has nothing to do with me. Do whatever you have to do. I have told you the truth. Now I really have to work."

I nodded absently, and five minutes after she'd gone I went out into the afternoon sun. There I stood another few minutes leaning on the Land Rover, thinking it through from every angle. Finally I climbed in behind the wheel and made my way slowly out of town along the Chancomayo Road. I turned right at the fork and climbed, bumping and lurching up the track, toward Liz Calder's dig.

I eventually came to the esplanade where they parked their Jeeps and trucks, and sat a little longer, looking at the massive, fifty- and hundred-ton rocks that formed the wall. How they did that was a mystery I could not solve, but who supplied the mayor with nuna miyu, and why, would be simpler.

I climbed out of the cab and walked down the path of broad, shallow steps. Pretty soon all the young archeologists in their denim shorts and straw hats began to appear, hunched over, scraping at the earth. I saw Liz. She was standing outside her tent, up against the megalithic wall, talking to a man in cream pants and a white shirt with the sleeves rolled up. His hat was also straw, but it was a Panama. They were both looking at some papers. There was a rock nearby which looked like it had once formed the base of a wall. I sat on it and watched them talk. Eventually Liz looked up and saw me, and froze, looking at me. The guy noticed and followed her line of sight. There was a moment of unreal stillness.

I stood and crossed the fifty paces that separated us, stepping over the occasional string that separated the zones of the dig. As I drew close Liz said, "What have you done with Charlie? We need her here."

I smiled blandly. "I threw her out of a plane over Madre de Dios." To the guy in the Panama I said, "You must be Pasqüal Bouc. I am Harry Baumb."

He was handsome in that French way that women like: scrawny with high cheekbones, dark eyes and dark, floppy hair. He looked like he smoked Gauloise and thought too much.

"I know who you are, Mr. Baumb," he said with only a trace of an accent. "I understand you have been upsetting people."

"Charlie was pretty upset at two thousand feet over the rainforest near Entre Ríos."

He gave an unflappable, Gallic smile. "You are joking, of course."

He stressed the "i" in "joking" instead of the "o." I offered him a soft grunt of a laugh and turned to Liz.

"I need to talk to you, urgently."

"I'm busy. You can see I am with Monsieur Bouc."

"Monsieur Bouc is welcome to sit in on our conversation. In fact, I'd like that. But I promise you are going to be really busy if we don't talk."

She glanced at Pasqüal but he raised his hands like she was aiming a gun at him.

"I am afraid I cannot stay. I have meetings in Cusco, then I must fly to Washington and then back to Genève." He pronounced it the French way, then went on, "And before that I must say au revoir to Amanda. So, c'est impossible."

I smiled.

"I hope one of the meetings is not with Alfredo, the mayor of San Julian. Mr. Bouc." He regarded me, blinking. I shifted from a smile to a grin. "He is also lying among the trees in Madre de Dios. It's getting pretty crowded down there."

"You have an unpleasant sense of humor, Mr. Baumb. I do not find this amusing."

"I have no sense of humor at all, Mr. Bouc, especially about child slavery. You ride with the devil, you're liable to get your ass burnt. You want to be part of this conversation, or do you want to go and have your meetings?"

He held Liz's eye for a moment, then looked at me and said, "Good afternoon, Mr. Baumb," and left.

Liz scowled at me. "Boy, you certainly know how to make an entrance, don't you?"

"Something they teach you in the SAS."

She frowned, confused. "Scandinavian Airlines?"

"Yeah, Liz, Scandinavian Airlines, let's go to your tent."

I followed her into the cool shade. I sat on a bentwood chair and she leaned her ass against her trellis table, where all her papers were mixed in with artifacts.

I gave her a lopsided smile. "It's not going to be that brief. You'd be more comfortable in a chair."

"I'm fine standing. Get on with it."

"Charlie is dead. So is the mayor."

Uncertainty crept across her face and ended in a twitch of a frown. "You said that. It's one of your inappropriate jokes."

"I killed them this morning, flying toward Alfredo's gold mine in Madre de Dios."

Now her eyes were wild under her frown. "What are you, some kind of psychopath?"

"Sometimes I wonder. How long have you been supplying him with nuna miyu?"

She leaned forward, scandalized. "What? Have I just slipped through the looking glass? What the hell are you talking about? Nobody knows how to make that shit!"

I laughed. "Oh no you don't! You gave Amanda Epstein the sample and Pasqüal Bouc has worked out how to synthesize it. She told me she stole it, but she was just protecting you, wasn't she? And to avoid years of trials and getting federal licenses, you've been testing it on Andean families working at Alfredo's gold mine and cattle farms. From what I have seen, it is one hell of a success."

It was like she had suddenly become frozen. She was rigid, leaning forward with her hands on her thighs. First she frowned, then her eyes started darting here and there, like they were looking for an explanation to what just happened to reality. Finally all she said was, "The mine?" I waited. Her face cleared. "You said Entre Rios? That was the town at the foot of the valley..."

"Yes, Elizabeth, that gold mine. You have so many you forget about this one?"

She shook her head. It was a sudden, urgent gesture. "But I didn't know! I had no idea! Alfredo must have done this without..."

"Won't wash. Where was he getting the drug from?"

"I don't..."

"I know you had an affair with Amanda Epstein." She stared at me, rigid. "Do you think the woman you had an affair with, who is a microbiologist, who is married to the Pasqüal Pharmaceutical Company of Munich, might be the one supplying Alfredo with the drug?"

Her face sagged. "No..." It was a whining, childlike sound. "No, not Amanda. No..."

"How then?"

The silence became oppressive. Outside, the desultory sounds of the dig failed to penetrate the silence. A voice here, a reply there, the scraping of a trowel; but they were somehow somewhere else, in another reality. I knew what she was going to say, and I didn't want to hear it. But she said it.

"Danny?"

I sighed. "Was that the plan? Kill the scapegoat right at the beginning so you can blame him for whatever comes up later?"

"No, no!" She looked around wildly. "But how else?"

"What are you saying, Liz? You think Danny Cooper had a lab in the woods somewhere? Alfredo told me specifically that it was you supplying him with the drug."

"Well he was lying!" Her voice had taken on a desperate edge. "I don't even know what the formula is. Amanda was..."

She stalled, hesitated. I said, "What? Amanda was going to what?"

"I didn't say that." She stood, went round the table, searching. "I was going to say that Amanda was the one who was interested in that aspect of it." She found what she was looking for and poured herself a trembling shot of whisky. She knocked it back and as she wiped her mouth I said, "So you're telling me Amanda was supplying Alfredo, pretending to be you?"

"No! Stop trying to confuse me! Stop putting words in my mouth!"

"Amanda was the one charged with getting the stuff analyzed so it could be synthesized. Isn't that what you were going to say?" She didn't answer. "She would get the Pasqüal Pharmaceutical Company of Munich to analyze it. It's not hard to manufacture. After all, the Incas did it right here. You don't require a big industrial facility, especially for the comparatively small amounts you needed. All you need is a small setup in the forest, maybe in the shelter of a large cave.

"And then, once that was set up, with the essential help of the mayor, you bought up the land in Madre de Dios. Everyone in the Peruvian Andes knows that Madre de Dios—the Mother of God

—is being raped by illegal gold miners. So all you have to do is move in on the racket with a handful of hard, seasoned mercenaries and three times the miners of any other illegal mine in the area. Because, not only are they numerous, they are absolutely obedient, work incessantly without complaining, and if the mine is raided, they are not afraid to die. Because their minds and their souls have been destroyed."

She didn't answer. She poured herself another drink and threw that one back after the first. She spoke as she set down the glass.

"I realize I look as guilty as hell. As you seem to be some kind of self-appointed judge, jury and executioner, I suppose now you are going to kill me. But I am telling you I knew nothing of this. And if I had known I would certainly never—never!—have gone along with it. I abhor slavery. It disgusts me!"

"Why did you buy the mine?"

She took a deep breath and released it as a deep sigh. Then she slowly lowered herself back into her chair.

"Amanda and I had become friends, close friends, and we were both facing the eternal problems you always face in any Latin American country, with bureaucracy, papers, delays...bribes!" She spent a moment turning the bottle in circles on the desk. "So we were both negotiating with Alfredo—the mayor—to extend our licenses. He was telling us he had good contacts in both Cusco and Lima who could speed things up for us—a lot. So obviously we asked, what would they want in exchange? He made a big show of saying, 'Nothing! Nothing! They'll help because you are my friends.'

"And then he whips out a map of a chunk of jungle in Madre de Dios which is going cheap. He says there is gold there and we can go five ways, me and him, Amanda and Pasqüal and the Pasqüal Pharmaceutical Company of Munich. We can run a legitimate mine and make millions."

She stared down at the tabletop for a while, then shook her head like she was bewildered.

"To be perfectly honest, I thought it was a lot of bullshit. I assumed that after a year or two we would discover that by some loophole of Peruvian law, we—Amanda, Pasqüal and I—did not own the land at all, and Alfredo was raising llamas there. I thought it was just a subtly disguised bribe."

"Your story is better than Amanda's. But you both leave something vital unexplained. There were only two people who had the possibility of supplying Alfredo with that drug, you and Amanda. If it wasn't you, then who the hell was it?"

In desperation she shook her head. "I don't know! Charlie?"

"I thought so, but I was wrong. It's a shame. I killed her for no reason."

"Then it has to be Pasqüal!"

"But Pasqüal operates here through Amanda, and you know it. She came here for one reason and one reason only. Te get her hands on the formula for nuna miyu. She got hold of it through you, had it analyzed by her husband, then had the formula synthesized. Once that was done they started having it manufactured out here, in secret, probably at her lab in the jungle. The mine was a way to test the drug and make some money into the bargain."

"I can't believe that."

"You can't believe it? Seriously?"

She rubbed her face in her hands and was very quiet for a while. Finally she looked up and she looked weary. She spoke quietly.

"You think I give one solitary fuck about that gold? You think I give a damn about the money? Well you're wrong, Harry. I don't give a fuck about money, gold, black powder, fame, honor... I care about two things." She raised her index and middle fingers. "Just two."

"Yeah?"

She gave a brief nod. "Come with me."

She stood and I followed her to the rear of the tent, where she pulled back a flap and exposed a small archway in the megalithic wall. She went through, holding the flap for me, and led me along a narrow passage that ended abruptly after about sixty or seventy paces. Here she stopped and turned to face me.

"Nobody has seen this except me, Amanda, Danny and now you. The team believe it is literally a dead end. I told them maybe we would excavate around it later on in the year. But right now it is just that, a dead end."

"So what's to see?"

"This."

She turned toward the wall that formed the cul-de-sac. It was composed of a single, massive hunk of granite. She leaned on a stone in the wall beside it, and then put all her weight against the stone that formed the end of the passage. Slowly, with a terrible grinding noise, it swung back on some kind of hinge and revealed a large, cavernous room, paved with stone slabs. I stepped inside and looked around. The walls were stone and the ceiling was stone, supported by megalithic stone columns. It was about twenty-foot square, and there was little in there other than some baskets and rugs, and what looked like a large, disk-shaped black stone in the center.

She spoke and her voice was sudden and loud in the darkness.

"You are one of four people who has been in here in the last twelve thousand years." She switched on a flashlight as she spoke. "That is when the door was sealed with adobe. This was the last place the victims stayed on earth, the night before they were sacrificed. That stone," she pointed to the black disk, "that is where they prepared the nuna miyu. The children would drink the tea, and it seems there were other psychotropic herbs involved which might have been inhaled or taken after the nuna miyu, and at dawn they would be led down that passage to join a procession which led them to the top of Apusupay. There, with their souls already consumed by Supay, their bodies would be hurled down into the Urubamba, symbolizing the great River of Life."

"From the same spot where Danny was pushed?"

She moved from the door to stand beside the black stone, looking down at it.

"Danny wouldn't take it," she said at last. "There is no way of knowing what kind of rituals they had, whether they chanted or sang, or danced. Because—" She looked up at me. "Because these were not Inca. We have no idea who they were, whether they became the Inca, or whether the Inca learned from them. But here is a fully formed, advanced civilization with highly developed mathematics and technology, cutting and moving huge megaliths great distances, who are occupying the Andes at least two thousand years before the first green shoots of civilization were supposed to have appeared in Mesopotamia."

"I don't understand..."

She gave a small laugh. "This is going to rock the archeological community. It is going to rock academia. It will shatter the mainstream view of human history. It has happened before and those academics were squashed underfoot by the establishment, but I am not going to let that happen to me. I am preparing my evidence very carefully indeed."

"Liz..."

She ignored me and crossed the room.

"See this basket here? There are five iron cups in it. The sixth is with a notary in Cusco. Each one of them has residue of nuna miyu in it, from eight to nine thousand years before the Iron Age began."

"Liz, what has this got to do with the gold mine?"

She smiled. "Nothing. That's my point, Harry. It has nothing to do with your problems. This, this is what I care about. You can run around chasing power and gold and killing people. I don't care. This—this! is what I care about. And when I am ready, I will write my article, and my book, and I will make my presentation at the Archeological Institute of America, and my evidence will be irrefutable."

I sighed loudly and it echoed in the dark corners of the stone chamber.

"OK, Liz, I get it, you made your point, but men, women and

children are dying, exploited as slaves. People are being murdered..."

The voice that answered me was not Liz's voice. It sounded slightly amused and seemed to come from above my head, among the stone slabs of the ceiling. It said:

"And most of them seem to have been murdered by you, Harry."

EIGHTEEN

D R. L IZ C ALDER DIDN'T BAT AN EYELID. Y OU'D ALMOST have thought she was expecting it. Her unblinking eyes remained on mine, as though she hadn't heard the voice at all.

I took a step to the side and turned. Amanda Epstein was in the doorway, her hands hanging by her side, barely more than a shadow, untouched by the light from Liz's flashlight.

"This," I said, "is the other thing you care about. It had to be both of you. There was nobody else, and neither of you could have done it alone. Your indifference to Danny's death, even though you both claimed to be infatuated with him, just clinched it, like your mention of a black powder you had supposedly never seen." I smiled and gave a small snort. "But what really sealed it for me was the way you both refused to implicate the only other person who could possibly have done it—each other. That kind of loyalty is rare, and it could only mean you were still a couple."

Amanda giggled from a face made invisible by shadows. "How clever of you, Mr. Baumb. What a shame you were not clever enough to avoid getting caught here with Liz and me, alone."

"Are you going to sacrifice me to the Supay, the way you did Danny?"

It was Liz who answered. "No, Harry, we're just going to kill you, plain and simple."

"A lot of people have tried. It hasn't gone too well for them."

Again Amanda laughed, invisible. Then she stepped into the light cast by Liz's flashlight, and from behind her back she pulled what looked like a pistol, but I knew it wasn't.

"This is a dart gun, Harry. It's used for shooting tranquilizer darts into large animals. The dart in this gun contains nuna miyu. You're lucky. Death will come easily to you. You won't suffer. Get on your knees."

"No," I said, feeling hot anger swell in my gut. "I won't die on my knees."

She smiled, and this time I saw her perfect white teeth glimmer.

"You know, the next time I tell you, you'll do it."

Questions flashed through my mind. How many darts did she have? How many feet per second did a dart travel? How good was her aim?

The light was poor and I took a step back and to the side again so I was deeper in the gloom, offering a more difficult target. I needed a plan and I could only think of one. Amanda raised the weapon in both hands. She was obviously enjoying herself and that was a good thing.

"I'm a good shot, Harry, and it really doesn't matter where I hit you, the drug will work the same. It might take a few seconds longer, but it will travel to your brain, and your soul will die."

Liz snapped, "Cut the dramatics, Amanda! This man is dangerous! Shoot him!"

Amanda was tracking me. I was moving steadily, from one side to another, backing toward the wall, inching closer to Liz, and all the while I was watching her stance, trying to sense the tension in her. The tension that would peak as she pulled the trigger. She said:

"I should have thought you'd enjoy a bit of castration, Liz.

Haven't you grown tired of this animal's macho antics over the last couple of days?"

Liz didn't answer. She was aware of what I was doing and strode suddenly toward Amanda, shining the flashlight directly at me, blinding me for a second. I heard her voice snap again, "Oh, shoot him for Christ's sake!"

I didn't wait.

I leapt and rolled across the floor. I heard the phut! And the crack of the dart as it hit the stone wall. And then the room exploded. I heard a scream. Liz's flashlight hit the floor and spun, hurling light and dancing shadows against the walls. I scrambled on all fours for the flashlight. There was another explosion. Screams of rage and fear. I grabbed the flashlight and spun it toward the entrance. Black shadows leapt and screaming voices echoed down the passage and rolled around the room.

But the room was empty.

Almost.

A black hulk lay near the doorway, motionless. I took the flashlight in my left hand and pulled the P226 with my right. Then I stood and stepped toward the motionless object on the floor.

It was Amanda Epstein, or what was left of her. She had a small entry wound in the back of her skull, but most of her face was an ugly mess on the twelve-thousand-year-old floor. She wasn't so easy to fall in love with anymore.

I picked up the dart gun that lay beside her, released the improvised syringe dart onto the floor and stamped on it. Then I collected up the five iron cups and ran down the passage following the disjointed echoes of the voices.

I burst through the flap and into Liz's tent. The trestle table had been overturned, the floor was covered in papers and broken artifacts, and there was another body on the floor. I hunkered down beside her and rolled her on her back. It was Charlie, Karina, her bright blue eyes staring unseeing past my head.

I felt a stab of pain and rage in my gut. Then she blinked and tried to focus on me.

"Jesus, that woman is punch like a mule."

"What the hell are you doing here? I told you to go to Cusco!"

"But I thought about it. Good for you I did. God, I feel sick with concussion..."

As she struggled to her feet I stepped out of the tent. All the young archeologists with their denim shorts and straw hats were standing, staring toward the lot where they parked their Jeeps. They looked unsettled. I heard the roar of an engine, and then the sound faded. Karina staggered out of the tent behind me.

I sighed. "Come on, we need to get out of here."

They all stood and stared at us as we made our way toward the Land Rover, with Karina hanging on my shoulder. One of the kids stepped forward, a blond guy in his mid-twenties.

"What the hell's going on?"

He yelled it from a distance. He didn't get too close. I stopped and looked at him.

"Dr. Calder has been experimenting with nuna miyu. It drove her crazy and she has shot and killed Dr. Epstein. Stay here, nobody leaves, I'm going to alert the authorities."

As we moved on a young woman's voice came after us, "What about the dig? Are we going to get paid? What about our credits?"

"Talk to the university," I snarled over my shoulder.

A male voice shouted, "Hey! Charlie! Who is this guy?"

We ignored him and collected Karina's stuff from the Merc, then drove slowly back to Angie's Hostal. I parked out front and helped Karina inside. The place was empty and Cas dropped what she was doing and ran to grab Charlie and help her to a chair. She glanced furiously at me and said, "What the hell?"

"Can it, Cas. I sent her to Helsinki. She didn't want to go. You want to do something useful, get her a shot of whisky, or brandy."

"Vodka," said Karina, with her eyes closed.

"Vodka, and seeing as your talking, you want to tell me where the hell you got a 9mm semiautomatic?"

"The glove compartment of the Mercedes. It was logical."

It was logical. I turned to Cas. "Has Liz been here?"

"Yeah, she came flying in like she had a hornet up her arse, ran upstairs, came rushing back down again and took off toward Cusco. Never said a word."

I nodded. "Don't let anything happen to Charlie. I'm going to get my stuff."

She watched in silence as I climbed the stairs. In my room I grabbed my things, dumped them in my bags and made my way down to the bar again. Cas was sitting holding Karina's hand and Karina was stretched out with her head resting on a cushion.

Cas said, "She has bad concussion..."

I interrupted. "She was punched by Liz Calder. She has mild concussion. It'll wear off in a while."

"You're going...?"

"I need to get her back home and out of harm's way. I need to finish my job and there is a hell of a lot of cleaning up to be done. But before any of that, there are some things I need to do here. I won't be long, a couple of hours." I jerked my head at Karina. "Meantime, keep her out of sight."

She frowned. "What are you going to do?"

"You don't want to know."

In the Land Rover, as I drove, I called the brigadier.

"Harry."

"I can confirm that things were as the senator thought. One target is down. There are at least two more. Dr. Liz Calder is right now on her way to Cusco and my guess is she's going to get a flight either to Geneva or Washington. If you can track her passport, that would be very helpful. Dr. Pasqüal Bouc is about an hour ahead of her. I don't know if they're going to travel together or whether they have separate destinations. But I need to know where they are both going."

His voice was cool. "That's not a problem, but why aren't you going after them, Harry? That would seem the logical thing to do."

"Yeah, it would be, if there weren't a field lab producing soul poison up here. And I really don't want the military-industrial complex getting their hands on that stuff."

"I see. Yes, all right."

"Meanwhile, you need to talk to the IT department. I need a special job done on the Pasqüal Pharmaceutical computer network."

I pulled up outside the Pachacutec Inca Hotel and went inside. The bald concierge smiled at me and bowed as I approached his desk. "Monsieur Baumb, what a pleasure to see you once more!"

I slipped him twenty bucks across the counter and said, "Dr. Epstein has asked me to come and collect some documents she left behind. She's at the field lab and there's no reception there, otherwise she'd call. Can you let me into her room?"

He made a regretful face and told me in French that he was desolated as he slipped the twenty back across the desk to me.

I smacked him only gently on the tip of his chin. His eyes rolled up and he sank behind the desk. I tied his wrists and his ankles and stuffed a napkin in his mouth, as well as another twenty and a ten in his pocket. I found the key to her room and sprinted up the stairs, opened the door and went in.

It was a suite, with a bedroom and a bathroom on the left and a living room straight ahead. The living room had a sofa and two armchairs facing a TV, and at the far end, by the window, there was a dining table with four chairs. The table had been pushed up against the wall and now held a computer, a stash of papers and a small, removable hard drive.

I found a suitcase in her wardrobe, gathered up the whole lot and dumped it in the case. Then left the room with a pillow under my arm. Before I left the hotel I put the pillow under the concierge's head. He was still sleeping peacefully.

I slung the case in the back of the Land Rover and headed out on the Chancomayo Road, took the right fork and started the long trundle up the dirt track toward the top of Apusupay. I passed the dig, down on my left, and briefly glimpsed the young diggers sitting in council.

Shortly after that, when the track forked again, I turned left and started the long, winding descent into the rainforest, along the ancient Inca, or pre-Inca paved path, toward the huge, looming wall of the mountainside, covered in the apparently impenetrable mass of creepers. I was soon swallowed by the tall trees where the towering canopy filtered the light, turning it green, mottled with sparse patches of sunlight that eventually disappeared altogether. And then the sheer face of the mountain reared up in front of me, wreathed in a vast tangle of vines and lianas. I drove on and plunged in among the green cascade, onto the vitrified black floor, with the array of tents spread out before me. Limpid light was filtering out through the windows and I could see two Wranglers parked over on the left. I killed the engine and climbed out.

A flap opened in the tent directly in front of me and three men stepped out. They didn't look real friendly and I made a mental note that two of them were missing. There should have been five, but I counted only three. I climbed down from the cab.

"Who's in charge here when Dr. Epstein's not around?"

"Me."

I hadn't seen them without their face gear before. This guy looked like he might have Indian roots. He was big, barrel-chested, with broad cheekbones and dark skin. He was poking a cigarette in his mouth and lit up while I answered.

"We need to talk. Where are the other two?"

He jerked his chin, indicating behind me. I turned and saw them. They were blocking my exit from the cave. They were in deep gloom and I could not make out their features. I turned back to the big guy. He spoke before I did.

"We know why you're here, and we ain't gonna let it happen."

I frowned. "Let what happen? Why do you think I'm here?"

"Amanda warned us you would be coming back to destroy the lab. It's not gonna happen."

I nodded. The lab was here. It was the only place it could be.

"What's your name?"

"Screw you."

"That's a nice name. Was that your mother's idea or your dad's?"

The two guys beside him stepped forward. The guy on his right also looked Indian. He had tattoos around his neck and on his arms. The other guy was suntanned, with bleached hair and a blond mustache. He also had tattoos on his forearms. They didn't look a lot like your stereotypic biochemists.

"OK, so you're tough guys and you don't know jack about biochemistry. We still need to talk." They didn't look real convinced. I shrugged and made an "I told you so" face. "Any of you guy know where Amanda is? No? You guys know where Dr. Calder is? How about Alfredo, the mayor? No? So how about we do this? You two," I indicated the two guys with tattoos, "frisk me for weapons while you three cover me from a distance, when you're satisfied I am not a threat, we go inside and I give you the good news. Sound reasonable?"

The three I could see glanced at each other. The big Indian jerked his chin at me and the tattooed two approached. I held up my hands.

NINETEEN

THE INDIAN GUY WITH THE TATTOOS ON HIS NECK found the Sig under my arm and extracted it with his left hand. He held it up and showed it to his boss. At the same time the blond guy with the moustache was hunkered down by my right leg, feeling the Fairbairn and Sykes fighting knife in my boot. The big boss was closing in, and so were the two guys behind me.

Disarming somebody who is holding a gun is extremely dangerous. Not only can you wind up making a real ass of yourself, you can wind up dead too. Three elements are essential: speed and clinical accuracy are two, but above all you need extreme aggression.

He had reached in my jacket with his left hand, holding my shoulder with his right. Now he extracted the weapon with his left hand and held it up, half turning away from me to show it to Screw You. I smashed my right palm into his wrist, and my left palm into the cannon of the Sig, levering it down so it was pointing at his temple. At the same time I slipped my right index into the trigger and pressed. The gun exploded and the 9mm slug smashed instantly into his skull, erupting from the far side of his head in a shower of blood and gore, but not much brains.

I knew I had two or three seconds. I didn't waste them. As he sagged and fell I took the P226 in both hands and directed it down at the moustache who was kneeling at my feet. He looked up in terror for less than a second, and the slug slapped through his forehead.

I didn't bother to aim at the two behind me. I fired roughly at the center of the nearest, who was just twelve feet away, and his pal turned, stumbling, to make a run for it. He took the next slug between his shoulder blades.

When I turned to face Screw You again, he was just two paces away, with a big ugly knife in his hand.

"Drop it."

I said it quietly, so he'd know I wasn't either shaken or stirred. He dropped the cigarette first and trod on it. Then he dropped the knife.

"Turn around, get on your knees and put your hands on your head."

He swallowed hard. "Please don't kill me. I was just following orders."

"I'm not going to kill you, Screw You. I need information from you. Now, turn around, on your knees and hands on your head. Don't make me tell you again."

He did as I said and I went to confirm the last two kills. He heard the shots and when I got back I told him, "It's just you and me now, Screw You."

His face went rigid and he looked at me sidelong. "That's not my name."

I smiled. It wasn't a nice smile. "So now you begin to see the importance of providing accurate information. What's your name?"

"John."

"OK, John, that's good. Now, let's go inside the admin tent. You lead the way."

He rose and walked the short distance, then pushed through the flap. I kept him covered and told him, "Take that chair, put it in the middle of the floor and sit with your back to me."

He did as I said and I moved up close behind him.

"I am going to ask you two questions. I know you know the answers, so for every time you hesitate or say 'I don't know' I am going to either shoot you somewhere non-lethal, or I am going to take a finger, a toe, a hand, a foot..."

I trailed off. His breathing rate had increased and he was swallowing a lot. When he spoke his voice was thick.

"How can you know I have the answers?"

"Because, John, you make the stuff and you store it." He went very still. I went on, "Where is the lab where you make the black powder?"

He spoke very deliberately. "It's not that simple. We manufacture it in the last tent. But we are always refining and improving it in the first and second tent, where you visited before."

I thought about the instruments I had seen there. "Hence all the fancy equipment."

"We are not just manufacturing it, we are trying to learn why it acts the way it does before we offer it to the wider market."

"You know I am going to check this."

"Yes. I am telling you the truth."

"OK, and where is the store?"

He pointed in the general direction of the last tent. "About one hundred kilograms in the lab, and then under a tarp outside another two hundred kilograms."

I nodded to myself. "OK, John, I have a couple more questions. The first is, who exactly is the wider market?"

He closed his eyes and took a deep breath. "The management in Geneva has a few interested parties. Naturally we were never allowed to know who they were, but we were offered huge bonuses if the drug became good enough for them to buy it."

It made sense. "OK, I buy that. What about the mayor's deliveries? He delivered the stuff to the mine and the farms?"

"We did. Sometimes it was me, sometimes it was Greg, the guy with the mustache."

"Where are the cattle farms?"

He pointed at the desk. "In the red ledger."

"You know what this black powder is?"

"Of course."

"OK, on your feet, lead the way to the storeroom."

As I followed him out of the tent and back across the black mirror of the floor I asked him, "You need to cook this stuff, like meth?"

He shook his head. "Not like meth. It has to boil, and then it has to be distilled..."

I interrupted him. "How do you make it boil? There is no electricity here."

He pushed aside the flap to the lab and said over his shoulder. "Propane canisters. We don't need high temperatures. Boiling point is all we need. Propane is fine for that..."

Again he trailed off and looked at me over his shoulder. We were in a long "room." It was lined with large, steel drums which were covered and had thick hoses feeding off into condensation chambers. He pointed at the large drums.

"We boil off the liquid. Most of the water vapor escapes into the air, a condensed extract runs off into the condensation chambers, and we are experimenting now with a spirit-based distillation. The black powder is what's left at the bottom of the drums. That just kind of has a deadening effect on people, but the distilled spirit seems to create some pretty freaky trips."

"Was it you who broke into Charlie's room and tried to kill her?"

"Yes."

"On whose orders?"

He turned to face me. "Pasqüal Bouc. He sent word through Amanda. Is Amanda dead?"

"Yes."

His bottom lip curled in and he turned away for a moment. Then he looked back at me. "You are going to kill me now?"

"Yes. I can't imagine a worse crime against humanity than the one you have helped to commit."

He gave a single nod. "I know. I did it for her. Can I take a cup of the powder, for the pain?"

"No, you face the reality of what you have done, and you face the reality of its consequences. Look me in the eye."

He tried, but he couldn't. He looked away and closed his eyes at the last moment. I shot him through the head.

I spent the next hour siphoning off the gasoline from the Jeeps and placing it, along with the spare gallon cans they had in the trunk, in the lab. I also dragged in the four hundred and forty pounds of the black powder they had stored outside. After that I dragged in six propane canisters that I found down beside the lab. I killed the burners that were making the drums of nuna miyu boil, and then reopened all the taps again. My final task, while the lab was filling up with gas, was to dump all Epstein's papers, and all the computers from the lab in with all the other crap from the lab.

Then I trailed a snake of gasoline from the lab to the great green curtain that hung down over the mouth of the cave. I'd picked up John's lighter earlier. Now I lit the trail of gas and drove out of the cave. I was ten seconds away, which is a long time when you're waiting for something imminent to happen, when the report came. It shook the air and made the Land Rover shudder. It sent a million birds flapping and screaming into the sky, above the canopy, and it set fire to some of the vines and the creepers that hung down from the mountain. That was good. This forest was too green to burn, but if there was fire inside the cave, then it would scour every last trace of nuna miyu from the face of the earth.

I got back to Angie's Hostal about twenty minutes later and found a familiar Nissan truck was parked outside. I swore violently under my breath, but couldn't say I was all that surprised. I climbed down from the cab, crossed the terrace and entered the saloon. He was up at the bar crooning at Cas, who looked strained and pale. Sitting at a table beside the door were three of his boys, looking vaguely bored. I said:

"Teniente Coronel de la Policía Nacional, Quillabamba, Atahualpa Flores. It is a pleasure to see you again. I was afraid I might leave without having the chance to say goodbye."

He regarded me throughout this speech with narrowed eyes but little more expression than that.

"You are leaving?" he asked, when I had finished.

"You advised me to go home, remember?"

He sneered. "What about your investigation?"

I ignored his sneer and smiled. "I am going to continue it from Washington. I have learned everything I needed to learn from San Julian."

"Dr. Calder telephone me. She is telling me you are molesting Dr. Epstein. I should come and arrest you."

I burst out laughing. "I am afraid Dr. Calder is a little bit angry with me. She um..." I looked at Cas behind the bar and grinned. "How can I say this politely? Dr. Calder got a little drunk last night and asked me if I would like to accompany her to her room. I declined because I already had an invitation from somebody younger and more beautiful."

Cas shook her head and muttered, "You son of a bitch."

Right on cue Karina appeared from the kitchen behind the bar. She smiled at me and said, "Hey, Harry. Are you ready? I've been waiting for ages."

I turned to the colonel. "Charlie and I are traveling back to the States together. My visit to San Julian was not a complete waste of time." To Karina I said, "Come on darling, help me get the things into the trunk."

As we grabbed her luggage and started carting it out I could hear the colonel asking Cas, "Is true? Last night Dr. Calder ask him this? And this little blonde one...?"

We dumped the stuff in the trunk and Karina clambered into the passenger seat. I leaned in and told her, "I'll be right back. Don't move."

As I walked in the door Cas was saying to the colonel, "She was as mad as a llama with a hornet up its ass. Furious. She grabbed her car and zoom! She was out of here. I suppose she went to Cusco. She didn't tell me. She just left."

He turned to me as I approached. "And Dr. Epstein? Where is she?"

I looked helplessly at Cas and shrugged. "The two doctors," I said with a laugh. "They are both workaholics. At this time of day they would normally be either at the dig or the field lab. But I must say farewell if I am to catch my flight, Colonel." I turned to Cas. "Cas, it's been a real pleasure. I wish it could all have been under different circumstances."

She came round the bar and hugged me. "Who knows," she said and gave me a kiss. "We might have made that three-night stand."

I smiled. "Keep that up and I'll be back next week."

I gave her another kiss and made for the door.

"Señor Baumb."

I stopped and turned. "Yes, Colonel?"

"Dr. Calder, she was pretty mad. She said you were a killer. Why she said this about you?"

"It's a New York expression, Colonel. It means that somebody is very attractive. Maybe that's what she meant."

"Have you seen the alcalde, Mr. Baumb? We been tryin' to call him on his phone and at his house. No answer."

I stayed very still, then retraced my steps till I was standing very close to him.

"I don't know why she called me a killer, Colonel. But any person using that term as an accusation, should be very sure of their facts. As to the mayor, well I heard somebody, maybe it was Dr. Calder or maybe it was Dr. Epstein, or perhaps it was Pasqüal Bouc, saying something about Mayor Alfredo Quispe spending a few days at his gold mine. I have no idea what that means. And I am pretty sure you have no idea what it means either, Colonel. Because if government forces, aided by the United States, should discover that Mayor Quispe and his friend, Teniente Coronel Atahualpa Flores, were involved in an illegal gold mine that employed child slaves, that would be a terrible thing indeed, wouldn't it?"

His eyes roved over my face. He looked like he wanted to peel me and roll me in salt, but he didn't say anything.

"I have finished my investigation, Colonel. What do you think I should do, reopen it, or leave?"

"I think you should leave, Mr. Baumb."

"No more questions?"

"No more questions."

"You have a good day, Colonel."

I climbed behind the wheel of the Land Rover and slammed the door. Karina watched me in silence. I fired up the V8 and followed the circle around to the Cusco Road. As I went I called the brigadier.

"Harry."

"Sir, any news?"

"Yes. Dr. Calder boarded a flight at Cusco International destined for Washington DC, London and then Munich."

"OK, good. You keep tabs on her there till I arrive."

His voice came back slightly sardonic. "Yes, sir."

"Sorry."

"Second target, Pasqüal Bouc, boarded an earlier flight for Washington. And before you start issuing instructions, we have people at the airport ready to meet them both and see what they do. My feeling is that they will hook up."

"I agree."

"By the way, that girl never showed up."

"No, she came back. She's with me now."

I heard the brigadier sigh loudly. "Harry, I trust she is not listening to this conversation."

"No sir. She's unconscious." She frowned at me. I shook my head briefly. "Sir, I need an urgent extraction. I am concerned a police colonel from Cusco may try to intercept our flight. I need a taxi that can get me to Washington ASAP."

"All right. Who is this colonel?"

"Teniente Coronel de la Policia Nacional, Quillabamba, Atahualpa Flores."

I heard him scribbling. "Did you do Spanish, Harry?"

"No sir, just what I picked up..."

"No, I didn't think so. Good. Anything else?"

"No, sir, that should cover it."

TWENTY

It was raining in DC. It was dark—as dark as it ever gets in DC. The light pollution created a dense orange ceiling over the city through which darkness seeped and filled the nooks and corners where the streetlamps could not reach. The road was black and slick, and the desultory cars that passed broke up the silver glow of the water and replaced it with foam.

I was sitting in a car on the corner of G Street NE and 13th Street NE. It was a big, double-fronted affair painted white, with big bow windows, set back from the sidewalk among lawns and gardens. Seven steps rose among cypress bushes to a big, friendly dark blue door with a shiny brass knob in the middle. The drapes were closed on all the windows, but the tech department and the tail who'd been sitting on them all day assured me that Dr. Liz Calder and Pasqüal Bouc were both inside, in the company of one man whom they had not been able to identify, another man whom they had identified as Pasqüal Bouc's attorney and two large bodyguards who had been French Special Ops.

I had snorted over the phone when the brigadier had told me that.

"French Special Ops. Sir? Isn't that a culinary skill? Like soufflé flambé? Or crêpe suzette?"

"Never underestimate your enemy, Harry."

"The French are not my enemy, sir. If they were, I would already have occupied Paris."

"Assume they are dangerous, Harry. What is your plan?"

I thought about it. "Go in, kill them, leave."

"What about the girl you brought back with you? Where is she?"

"On her way back home in Finland."

"Fine. Let me know when it's done and we'll send in the cleaners."

I hung up and climbed out of the anonymous Toyota Corolla, hunched into my shoulders and crossed the wet road, with spatters of cold rain pecking at my face. I had a clipboard in my hand and I was wearing the uniform of an MPDC sergeant. I opened the cold, wrought-iron gate and climbed the seven steps to the front porch. There I rang the bell. The drapes twitched on my right but I ignored them. A moment later I heard a door open and close. Then the front door opened and I was looking at a huge guy in a suit. He had a broken nose and a jaw like a megalithic Inca lintel. He opened his mouth and a noise came out that sounded like "Yah?"

I showed him my badge. "Sergeant Jones, Metropolitan Police, District of Columbia. I need to speak with Mr. Bouc."

The Mega Hominid opened its mouth again and said, "Ee is not avelabal now."

I said, "Oh, OK, um..." and as I said it I rammed the clipboard into his throat, breaking his windpipe. I stepped in quick and lowered him to the floor with difficulty. Once there I slipped the Fairbairn and Sykes from my boot and slipped it in fast behind his left collarbone. He bled out internally in a couple of seconds. So much for dangerous enemies.

I stood and looked around. There was a door on the right which suggested a living room, and another on the left which suggested either a dining room or a study. I opted for the living room and opened the door.

It was large, comfortable and expensively furnished. The TV was on and there was a fire burning in the grate. A man in his thirties was sitting in an armchair, frowning at me. He had on the same kind of suit as the giant in the hall. He said, "Oo are you?" with a pronounced French accent. I showed him my badge.

"Sergeant Jones, Metropolitan Police, District of Columbia. I am looking for Mr. Bouc. Your colleague said he was in here."

The frown turned into a scowl as he stood. "Monsieur Bouc is not in ear. Ee is in a meeting and ee cannot be disturbed!"

He came toward me and I entered the room pointing back over my shoulder.

"Your colleague is very dead," I said, which made him pause long enough for me to kick him in the balls, break his windpipe and administer the same kind of peaceful departure I had given his friend.

Thirty seconds later I stepped back into the hall and crossed it to what I figured now was the study. I had my P226 in my hand as I opened the door and went inside.

They were there, seated around the fire with drinks in their hands. They all looked up as I came in, and they all looked astonished. Pasqüal Bouc got to his feet and I trained the Sig on him.

"Don't bother, they're dead, and your house will be suffering telephone and WiFi problems for the next half hour. If I were you, I'd sit down, because as long as you're standing, I really want to shoot you."

He sat. I smiled at Liz.

"The kids were all asking for you. I told them you might not be back for a while. Poisoning people and using them as slaves is still frowned upon in this country."

She didn't answer so I turned to the two men on the sofa. The one on my right was a heavyset man in his forties, with very black brows and slightly purple lips.

"You must be Morris Leadbetter, attorney at law."

He wet his lips. "I don't know what you think you're doing, Sergeant, but this is a house invasion and you…"

I cut him short. "I was invited in by the dead behemoth in the hall. Also, I am not a police sergeant. I have a question for you, Mr. Leadbetter. Do you actually know what these people have been doing?"

"I don't have to tell you a damned thing."

I turned to the man next to him. "That's the thing with attorneys. They always have this idea that the worst thing that can happen to you is to get prosecuted. But there are much worse things, aren't there, Senator Ortega? Like having your soul consumed by a daemon, for example."

"I know this looks bad, Harry, but it is not what you think."

I laughed. "Come on, Randy! You really thought I wouldn't get it? Your first hit man was so stupid he posed as Danny's brother, said his and Danny's dad had met me in the army. So who knew I was looking for Danny? The brigadier, the colonel, you... And then the guy you sent to San Julian. I've got to hand it to you. That was pretty fast work." I looked at Bouc. "Did you use the company jet? He called me Henry. He said he was Don Gardner, from the Office of Internal Accounting at the Pentagon. That was stupid. Because the only people who knew I was Henry were, again, the brigadier, the colonel and you. And the Office of Internal Accounting? Really? You were bragging, letting me know that you were not afraid of the H-bomb, right?"

He didn't answer. I turned to Liz again. "There are a couple of things I am not totally clear on. Help me out. Your passion, your consuming passion, was the dig, being able to reveal what you had learned about these people who came so long before the Incas."

She was nodding. "That is still true."

"But you know there would be strong political opposition. So you tried to enlist the help of Edwin Cooper through his son, Danny."

"Yes."

"But he turned you down."

"We rowed. The naïve little shit wanted to make his name

without his father's help. I tried everything to make him under-stand that archeology does not work that way. Discovering amazing things is not enough. If you are going to go up against the established order you need political backing. You need spon-sors, people who carry weight, and money."

"So you turned to your old pal, Randy."

"Not exactly. Randy was interested in what I was doing. He always had been. But when he learned that I might have stumbled across the nuna miyu he started telling me that his support, and that of some other very influential people, could be provided at a price."

I cut in, "And that price was to let Dr. Amanda Epstein and Pasqüal Bouc have a sample of the nuna miyu so that they could synthesize it."

"Yes."

"At first you said no, and tried to work on Danny, but in the end Amanda got to you."

"Yes. She is the only person I had ever really loved."

"Yeah." I sighed. "John at the lab felt the same way."

There was a sudden screech from the sofa. Pasqüal Bouc was on his feet again, spitting as he spoke.

"I told you! I told you, you stupid woman! If you 'ad accepted our offer from the start, none of this would 'ave been necessary! You would 'ave your honor and your glory! You would have Amanda! And we would have the nuna miyu! You stupid, stupid woman!"

"But you would own me!" she screamed back at him.

"I already own you! You fucking stupid!"

"Cut it out," I said quietly. "And you sit down. Next time I'll shoot you."

He sat, scowling at Dr. Calder.

"I saw a gold mine in Madre de Dios," I said, "where about seventy-five women and children, and about twenty-five men, were working as slaves, being fed nuna miyu to make them compliant and obedient. I later spoke to John, at the lab, and he told me that he was doing this on your orders, all of you, and that it was down to him to deliver this stuff to the mine and to the farms."

"Do not answer that!" It was Leadbetter.

"I have to tell you that John has turned state's evidence, along with the other lab workers, and so have the motley crew of South African desperados from the mine."

Liz snapped, "You said you'd killed them!"

"And you believed me. You seriously think I'd kill my prime witnesses?"

That had them all glancing at each other. I went on.

"So you got together and decided the way to go was to use Mayor Alfredo Quispe's farms to test the drug, and you," I pointed at Pasqüal, "thought it would be a better idea to move into Madre de Dios and get yourselves a gold mine."

He shook his head. "It was not my idea!"

Leadbetter screamed, "Pasqüal! Shut up! Shut up!"

"I can tell you everything! I know everything! The gold mine was Leadbetter's idea. Him and Randy. They came up with the idea together! I will sign a deal with the DA! I have connections!"

Leadbetter staggered to his feet and started beating Pasqüal with his attaché case, screaming at him, "Shut up! Shut up, you fool! Shut the fuck up!"

I shot him through the head. His head whiplashed and a big ugly stain splatted against the wall behind the sofa. He slumped onto the floor and laid his head on Pasqüal Bouc's lap. Pasqüal screamed like a girl and started pushing at him with his hands, trying to get out from under him. As he rose to his feet, Leadbetter dropped to the floor and I shot Pasqüal Bouc in the head too. He looked momentarily shocked. Then his legs wobbled and he tipped over the chair he'd been sitting in.

Dr. Liz Calder and Senator Randy Ortega sat very still, staring at me. I said:

"Here is where it all began, with Senator Randy Ortega and

Dr. Liz Calder, and their interest in the mysteries of South America's past. Why did you do it, Randy?"

He didn't answer. I shrugged. "I know why Liz did it. She told me. Nothing was more important for her than the dig. And if the price for that dig was the souls of hundreds of people, so be it. But you? You betrayed your friend, your people, your office...for what?"

"Gold," he said simply. "And do you realize what that powder is worth to the military industrial complex? That stuff can be weaponized..."

"Could have been," I said. "There is not a trace of it left. The iron cup has been recovered from the notary in Cusco, and all six cups have been cleaned and are now in a private collection, The lab has been destroyed. The mine has been closed and the farms are being closed down as we speak. Not a trace of nuna miyu remains on this planet. So, Randy, it can never be weaponized."

I shot them both, called it in to the brigadier and left the house. It was still raining as I loped across the road with my collar raised against the cold. The autumn was coming, closing in.

As I drove away the cleaner vans were pulling up outside the house. I headed for the airport, driving a little too fast. I was tired. Tired in my bones. Tired of humanity and its dark, cruel ways. Tired of my own cruelty. In my mind I went through all the possible loose ends. The Pasqüal Pharmaceutical Company of Munich had been hacked by Cobra hackers and all the files they had relating to nuna miyu had been corrupted or deleted, and sanitized evidence of the firm's involvement in illegal gold and slave trading in Peru had been fed to the German police, the Swiss police and Europol.

There was not a trace, I told myself. Not a trace left on earth.

I made the airport, returned the car and was fast-tracked onto the waiting air taxi. I settled into a soft, leather seat at a table as the door hissed closed and asked the stewardess for a large Macallan. She brought it to me as we taxied toward the runway and I pulled my cell from my pocket and called my home number. It rang twice and a delicate voice said, "Yes?"

"I'll be in New York in less than an hour, home in maybe an hour and a half."

"I am making creamy salmon soup and sautéed reindeer. It is typical Finnish food, and very good."

"I can't wait."

I closed my eyes as the world fell away beneath me, thinking about that poor damned reindeer.

Don't miss SWEET RAZOR CUT. The riveting sequel in the Harry Bauer Thriller series.

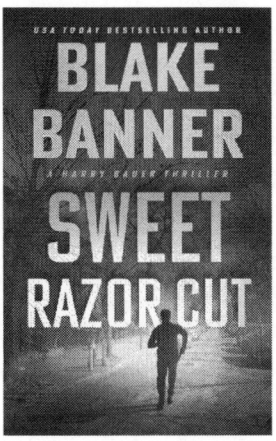

Scan the QR code below to purchase SWEET RAZOR CUT.

Or go to: righthouse.com/sweet-razor-cut

NOTE: flip to the very end to read an exclusive sneak peak...

DON'T MISS ANYTHING!

If you want to stay up to date on all new releases in this series, with this author, or with any of our new deals, you can do so by joining our newsletters below.

In addition, you will immediately gain access to our entire *Right House VIP Library,* which includes many riveting Mystery and Thriller novels for your enjoyment!

righthouse.com/email

(Easy to unsubscribe. No spam. Ever.)

ALSO BY BLAKE BANNER

Up to date books can be found at:
www.righthouse.com/blake-banner

ROGUE THRILLERS
Gates of Hell (Book 1)
Hell's Fury (Book 2)

ALEX MASON THRILLERS
Odin (Book 1)
Ice Cold Spy (Book 2)
Mason's Law (Book 3)
Assets and Liabilities (Book 4)
Russian Roulette (Book 5)
Executive Order (Book 6)
Dead Man Talking (Book 7)
All The King's Men (Book 8)
Flashpoint (Book 9)
Brotherhood of the Goat (Book 10)
Dead Hot (Book 11)
Blood on Megiddo (Book 12)
Son of Hell (Book 13)

HARRY BAUER THRILLER SERIES
Dead of Night (Book 1)
Dying Breath (Book 2)
The Einstaat Brief (Book 3)
Quantum Kill (Book 4)
Immortal Hate (Book 5)
The Silent Blade (Book 6)
LA: Wild Justice (Book 7)

Breath of Hell (Book 8)
Invisible Evil (Book 9)
The Shadow of Ukupacha (Book 10)
Sweet Razor Cut (Book 11)
Blood of the Innocent (Book 12)
Blood on Balthazar (Book 13)
Simple Kill (Book 14)
Riding The Devil (Book 15)
The Unavenged (Book 16)
The Devil's Vengeance (Book 17)
Bloody Retribution (Book 18)
Rogue Kill (Book 19)
Blood for Blood (Book 20)

DEAD COLD MYSTERY SERIES
An Ace and a Pair (Book 1)
Two Bare Arms (Book 2)
Garden of the Damned (Book 3)
Let Us Prey (Book 4)
The Sins of the Father (Book 5)
Strange and Sinister Path (Book 6)
The Heart to Kill (Book 7)
Unnatural Murder (Book 8)
Fire from Heaven (Book 9)
To Kill Upon A Kiss (Book 10)
Murder Most Scottish (Book 11)
The Butcher of Whitechapel (Book 12)
Little Dead Riding Hood (Book 13)
Trick or Treat (Book 14)
Blood Into Wine (Book 15)
Jack In The Box (Book 16)
The Fall Moon (Book 17)
Blood In Babylon (Book 18)
Death In Dexter (Book 19)
Mustang Sally (Book 20)

A Christmas Killing (Book 21)
Mommy's Little Killer (Book 22)
Bleed Out (Book 23)
Dead and Buried (Book 24)
In Hot Blood (Book 25)
Fallen Angels (Book 26)
Knife Edge (Book 27)
Along Came A Spider (Book 28)
Cold Blood (Book 29)
Curtain Call (Book 30)

THE OMEGA SERIES
Dawn of the Hunter (Book 1)
Double Edged Blade (Book 2)
The Storm (Book 3)
The Hand of War (Book 4)
A Harvest of Blood (Book 5)
To Rule in Hell (Book 6)
Kill: One (Book 7)
Powder Burn (Book 8)
Kill: Two (Book 9)
Unleashed (Book 10)
The Omicron Kill (Book 11)
9mm Justice (Book 12)
Kill: Four (Book 13)
Death In Freedom (Book 14)
Endgame (Book 15)

ABOUT US

Right House is an independent publisher created by authors for readers. We specialize in Action, Thriller, Mystery, and Crime novels.

If you enjoyed this novel, then there is a good chance you will like what else we have to offer! Please stay up to date by using any of the links below.

Join our mailing lists to stay up to date -->
righthouse.com/email
Visit our website --> righthouse.com
Contact us --> contact@righthouse.com

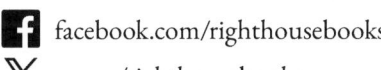 facebook.com/righthousebooks

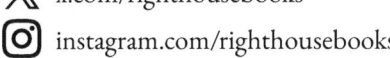 x.com/righthousebooks

instagram.com/righthousebooks

EXCLUSIVE SNEAK PEAK OF...

SWEET RAZOR CUT

CHAPTER 1

I OPENED MY EYES TO THE DARK, AWARE THAT somebody was there. I remained very still, breathing steadily, like I was sleeping. The dark was too dense. I shifted my eyes to the window. The drapes over the window were closed. I had left them open. The air was still, close, immobile.

I slipped from the bed and hunkered down beside it, below the window. I listened. There was only the heavy stillness of the small hours. The darkness was thick, like a physical thing. I stayed low and moved to the end of the bed. I sensed a breath but could not locate it or gauge the distance. I peered around the end of the bed. Where the bedroom door was, the darkness was less dense and I could sense rather than see that the door was open and the presence was gone.

I stood and moved quickly to the door, flattened myself against the wall, waited to a count of three, listening to the silence, hunkered down and peered out onto the landing. There was nothing there.

I moved fast to my bedside drawer, pulled it open and took out my Sig. I stepped back out onto the landing. My eyes were getting accustomed to the dark and I moved on swift, silent feet to the top of the stairs. Light from the stained-glass window on the landing touched the stairwell with ghostly light. A slight shadow moved across it. I ran down three steps at a time, no longer trying to be silent, bellowing, "*Freeze or I'll shoot!*"

I reached the second floor and in the dim half-light saw that the bedroom doors and my study were all open. One by one I checked the rooms, starting by the stairs and moving along the landing to the left. I saw nothing and heard nothing, but when I came to the last bedroom, farthest from the stairs, I heard the soft brush of fabric behind me. I dropped and swung round. A shadow, a ghost of a shadow, moved from the door and slipped silently down the stairs.

I sprang after it, bellowing, "*Stop! Stop, goddammit!*"

The figure was no more than eight feet ahead of me. In a single, fluid movement it vaulted the banisters and had suddenly gained a flight on me. I jumped down to the landing, hurled myself around to the next flight and saw the empty entrance hall touched by the dim, amber glow from the silent street outside. The front door was open and I could see the soft, yellow light of the streetlamps on the sidewalk, the black stencils of the autumn branches, the motionless, sleeping cars with their black windshields like dead eyes lost in dreams.

The presence was gone. I closed the door and checked the living room, the dining room, and the room I had set aside as a small library; and at the back of the house I checked the kitchen and the bathroom. But I found what I knew I would find: nothing.

A ninja? I smiled and shook my head. They don't make ninjas like that anymore, if they ever did. Shaolin? Unlikely. There was more legend than fact surrounding both the ninjas and the Shaolin monks, and where the ninjas had been trained assassins, the Shaolin monks were firmly rooted in Buddhist and Taoist principles, and they didn't go around killing people.

On the other hand, he hadn't killed me, where he could have if he had wanted to.

I went to my living room, leaving the lights off, and poured myself a stiff Macallan. Then I sat in my armchair beside the cold fire, looking at the street outside and thinking. The person I had just chased had skills beyond mere fighting abilities. We had not exchanged a single blow, yet I knew he could have taken me out at any time. I probably wouldn't even have known I was dead. He had a level of self-control that was well out of the ordinary, that you rarely found even in the Far East, let alone the West. That kind of control came from years of meditation, training mind and body to work together.

I could not think of anyone I knew of with that kind of training. Even my Jeet Kune Do instructor, Zamudio, didn't have that kind of training.

So questions: Who was he? And, also, what was his purpose?

Then, outside, on the far sidewalk, I saw a figure. My skin went cold and prickled. It seemed to materialize out of the shadows, an ink-black silhouette. It took a few steps, stopped when it was directly opposite me and, after a fraction of a second, turned and stared right at me, as though the eyes could penetrate the darkened glass right into my darkened living room. I felt a hot jolt in my belly, a strange mix of rage and fear. I sprang to my feet and ran to the front door. I wrenched it open and went out onto the stoop. There was nobody across the street on the far sidewalk. There were the dark, shifting shadows of the plane trees and the sleeping cars. And the silence of the small hours.

I went back inside and closed the door. I checked every inch of the house from my bedroom down to the kitchen and the gym in the basement, but found nothing of any interest. By then it was half-past five, so I went for a run, keeping my eyes peeled, watching the pre-dawn traffic, and the headlamps through the grainy haze of gray-blue light.

I ran a zigzag: west along 128th as far as Malcolm X Boulevard, then north a block, and east along 129th as far as Madison Avenue, then north a block to 130th, and so on until I came to the guys setting up the fruit and vegetable stall outside McDonald's on 132nd. When I got there I turned east and started zigzagging my way back toward James Baldwin Place. I figured the track was a couple of miles and took it easy, shadowboxing, sprinting, changing pace and weaving, and ducking and diving as I went. In a little under fifteen minutes I got home. I went down to the gym and worked out for an hour on the weight machines and the sack, showered and went up for breakfast. All the while I was allowing my unconscious mind to work on the two questions I had, distracting my chattering intellect and waiting for the answers to come. But nothing happened and I came to no brilliant realizations. There was a bland normality to the day.

Except that somebody had come to visit me between three and four in the morning. He was exceptionally skilled, could have killed me at any moment if he had wanted to, but instead he had left, taking care to let me know he was watching me.

Who was he? What was his purpose?

I ate a breakfast of strong black coffee and wholegrain rye toast in the kitchen, watching the golden morning yawn and stretch across my green lawn as the starlings began to emerge in small, hesitant clouds, silenced by the bulletproof glass of my windows. They hovered around the trees, fluttering, and were suddenly sucked back in again, like the film of their short lives had been suddenly run in reverse. Then they erupted in a huge shimmering cloud and soared, circling the blue dome of the sky in wild, synchronized abandon.

That made me smile.

I picked up the phone and called the brigadier as I sipped the last of my coffee.

"Yes," he said.

"Sir, it's Harry."

"I'm aware of that. I was just thinking about you. Synchronicity."

"Yeah? I was wondering if you had decided to put me out to pasture. You didn't like how I handled San Julian?"

"Not at all, Harry. Don't get sensitive on me, that's all I need.

I just thought you could use a rest, and it wouldn't be a bad thing if the world saw a little bit less of you for a while."

"Was that your idea or the colonel's?"

"Fifty-fifty."

"For how long?"

"Well, oddly enough, as I say, I was thinking of you this morning. I'll come and pick you up about seven. We'll have dinner and a chat."

I nodded, though he couldn't see me. "I had a visitor last night."

He didn't miss a beat. "Do you need the cleaners?"

"No."

Now he sounded surprised. There was a short pause while he took it in. "Really? What happened?"

"I woke up at about four. I could sense someone in the room. I always sleep with the drapes and the windows open, but they were closed. I went after whoever it was down the stairs. I saw their shadow a couple of times but that was all. They were very fast and very agile. When I got down to the front door it was open and there was no sign of them, but a little later I saw them across the road, looking at the house."

"Could you make out any features?"

"No. He was a shadow. He was very silent, with extreme self-control and exceptional training."

"What about your alarm system?"

"He didn't trigger it. But it's not all that sophisticated."

"Why not, Harry? It should be."

"Yeah, I know." I looked into the bottom of my empty cup. "But then I'd be one of those guys with a cutting-edge security system."

"Like me."

"No, not like you, sir," I said and sighed. "One of those other guys."

"We'll discuss it when I see you later."

"Yes, sir."

I stood and went to the entrance hall to check the alarm. I hadn't checked it before because I knew what I was going to find. The circuits had all been fried, probably by an EMP. They were no great mystery. Given a little know-how and a decent ion lithium battery, anyone could put together a functional EMP device with a range of about six feet; enough to blow out most alarm systems. Some basic lock-picking skills and you're inside.

The brigadier was right. My home security and my alarm system were not up to par. But I was right too. I didn't want to be that guy who puts so much time and energy into protecting his life that in the end he has no life left to protect. Besides, I had always trusted a good iron deadbolt and a solid baseball bat a hundred percent more than an electronic circuit. You can't fry a deadbolt with a homemade EMP. So I took a stroll down 5th Avenue to West 125th and, somewhat reluctantly, bought four big, iron deadbolts. I didn't really need to keep anybody out, I told myself. What I really wanted was to hear them coming in.

I got home and fitted the deadbolts to the kitchen door and the front door, one at the top and one at the bottom. After that I took a drive to Zamudio's place in the Bronx. He had a house at the corner of Screvin Avenue and Barret, right by Pugsley Creek. It was a three-storey redbrick and he'd knocked his ground floor into the garage and converted it into a large gym. From age thirteen he'd travelled the world studying everything from boxing and shotokan to ITF Tae Kwon Do and Wing Chun. But after he befriended Dan Inosanto in California, and started studying Jeet Kune Do with him, he decided he had found what he called the ideal synthesis.

"Be like water, my frwend," he used to say, mimicking Lee's accent, "and honestly expwess yourself."

I had never quite grasped how beating seven bales of shit out of somebody was honestly expressing yourself, but Lee had understood it, and apparently so had Zamudio. I had not got there yet.

I pulled up in the quiet, leafy street beside the park and left the TVR in the shade of the trees. He had his garage door open and I could see him inside doing two-finger push-ups. He was in his mid-fifties, but he was still the fastest, strongest, most explosive fighter I had ever encountered.

He jumped to his feet and smiled at me.

"What happened?"

I made a question with my face and he pointed at it.

"You look worried. Something's eating you. What is it?"

I smiled and went to sit on the bench below the coat rack, but he was shaking his finger at me. "Don't sit down. Take off your leather and start warming up. You can work and talk."

"I had a visitor last night," I said as I shrugged out of my jacket.

"Did you talk to him?"

I laughed and shook my head, then started stretching my neck. "In fact, the thing that most struck me about him was his silence."

"Yeah? Silence?"

"He moved like his feet weren't touching the ground."

"That's a lot of leg muscle control."

"Yeah." I thought about it while rolling my shoulders. "He was like a Hollywood ninja. Like a shadow."

Zamudio laughed. "He really impressed you, huh?"

"Yup. He could have killed me any time he wanted to. He came into my room and closed the window and the drapes without waking me."

"So how come he didn't kill you while you were sleeping?"

"I don't know. I awoke when he was leaving the room. I can't figure what he wanted."

I bent and pressed my head against my knees. Zamudio said, "You said he was silent. So your instinct woke you up. But what I am asking you is, how come he didn't kill you? Focus on that."

I stood erect and let myself slide down into the splits.

"I've been turning it over in my head all morning. The only thing I can come up with is that he was more interested in telling me something, letting me know he was there," I paused, lingering on the thought, "and he could return anytime he wanted to."

He snorted. "Truly powerful generals hide their strength. Weak generals make a big display. What makes him want to show you his strength? Why does he warn you in advance?"

I looked up at him and nodded. "That's exactly what I was wondering. And I can only think of one answer."

He jerked his head toward the rack of dumbbells. "Weights. You work, biceps, sixty seconds fast as you can. I'll tell you what I think."

I started hammering with twenty-two pounds in each hand while he spoke.

"Some time in the past you hurt this man, you broke him and humiliated him, or somebody he cared about. Now he wants to kill you, but first he wants you to know he is better than you, stronger, better trained, more dangerous. Killing you is not enough, he needs to humiliate you first."

I relaxed my arms. "Yeah, that makes sense."

"OK, shoulders, sixty seconds, fast as you can."

I began to lift, two lifts a second, arms outstretched to the side. Zamudio kept talking.

"So his weaknesses are first of all that he is emotionally compromised and sees only what he wants to see, and second he sees himself as more powerful than he is. In fact he is weak, and his weakness is that he needs you. He needs your admiration." I let out a noise born of pain and let my arms drop. He jerked his head at the weights machine. "OK, triceps and legs, then we spar for a while."

We worked out for another couple of hours, during which he kept telling me to think with my belly. I kept telling him that was bullshit. "You think with your brain, Zamudio. You digest with your belly."

He danced, ducked and dived. "Who is bruised and hurting?"

"Me," I said, trying to follow his movements.

He feinted with a backhand to my head and as I weaved away

he kicked my feet from under me and I landed with a *whoosh!* on my back. He leaned over me and wagged a finger.

"The brain is too slow. You have to think with your belly. Your belly is the center of your universe. If you think, 'What is he going to do now? He has his right foot forward so maybe he will strike with a straight right...,' by the time you have finished thinking I have destroyed you twenty times over. You have to *feel* with your belly, and respond, without words in your head." I reached up and he pulled me to my feet. "What have you done about this intruder?"

"I bought big, iron deadbolts for the doors."

He nodded. "Good."

Bruised, stiff and with strained leg muscles I made my way back to Manhattan, trying to think with my belly.

CHAPTER 2

AT SEVEN O'CLOCK THE BRIGADIER TURNED UP IN A dark Bentley Flying Spur V12. I trotted down the steps of the stoop, the chauffeur opened the door for me and I climbed in beside the brigadier. He was in a black evening suit with satin lapels and a bowtie. He eyed my business suit with an arched eyebrow and sighed softly, but he didn't say anything.

As we pulled away he asked, "Have you reviewed your security system?"

"Yup."

"A good attack is the best defense, we all know that, Harry. But the basis of a good attack is a solid defense."

"I know. Believe me, if anyone tries to get in again, I'll know all about it, and so will they."

He regarded me a moment. "You've set up tripwires attached to bottles and tin cans, haven't you?"

"No, sir." As I settled back I asked, "Is the colonel not joining us?"

He raised an eyebrow at me and we didn't talk all the way down Park Avenue until we turned into West 51st. Then he said, "Freud said that women were the Dark Continent and after a lifetime of research he had failed to understand them. I have to say I am with him. Most incomprehensible is their singular bad taste in men." He gazed at me a moment. "I don't mean to be offensive by saying that, Harry. I was married five times and never understood what any of them saw in me."

We went to Gallagher's, on West 52nd. It was one of those dim, dark wood and very white linen restaurants that the brigadier liked. I confess I like them too, and the steaks are like nothing on earth, unless you go up to Wyoming, hunt yourself a bison and cook it over an open fire. We pulled up outside the restaurant and strolled inside. The maître met the brigadier with a bow and led us to a booth.

"Your usual table, Brigadier."

"We'll have two vodka martinis while we look at the menu." We sat and to me he said, "You don't need to leave New York on this job, so you won't be able to blow anything up." He smiled. "Jane told me to make a point of telling you that."

Colonel Jane Harris was the head of operations at COBRA and frequently complained that I resorted too often to explosives to get a job done. She had not been on the scene since she was abducted by Russian Mafia and barely escaped with her life. I had saved her life and, for some reason only a woman would understand, she had held that against me ever since.

"What's the job?"

"It's fairly straightforward, but it has to be done right. Marco Benini, the capo of the Benini family."

I frowned. "That's law enforcement. Why don't the Feds take care of it?"

"They came to us. They can't touch him. Quite aside from his friends in high places..."

I interrupted, "Blackmail?"

"Yes. He has dirt on just about everyone and anyone who counts in this city. But aside from that he has been very careful and whether you follow the money, the blood or the connections, they all lead to a dead end and fall well short of him. All the Feds have is rumor and circumstantial evidence, and evidence which, though it is highly probative, was illegally obtained and therefore inadmissible in court. I admire much about the USA, Harry. But that particular quirk of your legal system is asinine. Thanks to it, Benini is untouchable."

The waiter brought the two martinis while another handed us our menus. We toasted and sipped. As I put down my drink I said, "Forgive me, sir, but there must be a thousand untouchable guys like Benini in New York. What makes him special?"

He took a deep breath. "Well, partly the fact that the FBI have asked for our help, which is a gesture of goodwill on their part, and we need a good relationship with them. But partly also because of his catalogue of crimes, and the fact that he is not so much expanding, as spreading."

"What's his portfolio?"

"White slaving from Eastern Europe. That is still a problem Poland refuses to address, and the European Commission turns a blind eye. They are more worried about whether Poland is going to destroy their dream of a Federal Europe than they are about the white slave trade which operates there. He is also involved in heroin and cocaine importation from Mexico, a large percentage of which is paid for in weapons. There is the usual drug selling here at home, and the murder and torture of rival gang members, especially in the Bronx. But perhaps the most heinous of his operations is the kidnapping of young girls in Portugal, Spain and Italy, to sell them in North Africa and the Middle East as brides for whoever can afford them."

"Yeah." I looked down at my martini and extracted the olive. "I saw a bit of that in Afghanistan, and other parts. They tell you it's a cultural thing. Trouble is, criticizing that culture can carry the death penalty."

"So, if Benini were to meet with an unfortunate accident, it would save the Bureau a lot of time and money."

"I'd be happy to oblige."

I turned my attention to the menu, but the brigadier cut in. "I suggest a lobster salad to start, with a glass of the house white, and a couple of rib-eye steaks and a bottle of *Muga*. All right?" I nodded and he called over the waiter, muttering, "I don't want to get sidetracked by the food."

I sat back as the waiter took away our menus and our order. "So this guy is in New York?"

"He has a mansion on the Esplanade in Pelham Manor. He follows a very strict routine, which may make life easier for you— or not. I am not sure. Every day at eight thirty AM his chauffeur drives him, and two of his boys, to his office at 530 Park Avenue. At five thirty the car returns, picks him up and takes him home."

"His office? He doesn't run his empire from a seedy strip club like every other self-respecting mobster?"

"Oh, no!" He gave a small laugh. "He has a small, but lucrative investment company called Benini Holdings, from which he invests in companies that invest in companies that invest in companies. Sometimes they are laundering operations, sometimes they are straight criminal operations—in jurisdictions where the States can't touch them. The point is he uses the Park Avenue company to tie his operations up in a miasma of holdings, umbrellas and investments so that he, personally, is completely removed from any criminal activity which may occur. And for good measure he has his attorneys right next door, a firm, incidentally, in which he holds a fifty percent share. The firm is Shawn Shave and Shearing."

"There has to be a pun in there somewhere."

He smiled. "I've been looking but I haven't found one yet. His attorney is Colin Shearing, the senior partner."

I peered doubtfully into my drink. It was half empty, though it might have been half full. "He follows that routine every day?"

"Like clockwork. My contact at the Bureau tells me very successful crime bosses often fall into that kind of routine when they get older. That's how a lot of them end up getting shot."

I thought about it, looking across the room at a couple talking quietly, affectionately, in the corner. They weren't worried about growing careless and getting plugged.

"It gets exhausting," I said, then turned to look at him, "always being on your guard."

"It does. So he has built up his security and allowed himself to fall into a routine. Very, very occasionally he goes abroad. But most of the time he just follows his daily rhythm. His car takes him home from the office at about five thirty every day, Monday to Thursday, but on Friday he goes to *L'Artigiano* on East 64th."

"An Italian restaurant."

"Correct."

"That's more like it."

"He dines while his boys sit at another table. Sometimes somebody joins him, usually it's one of his attorneys, or a broker, and at half past nine his car takes him home."

The waiter came with the lobster salad and the wine waiter poured us two glasses of the house white. Once he was gone the brigadier said, "It should be a very straightforward job."

"You keep saying that," I said around a forkful of lobster.

"Yes, well, last time you undertook a simple, straightforward job I seem to remember you blew up half of the Andes. Shortly before that you blew up all of New Mexico and a little before that I believe you actually expanded the Black Sea by several miles."

He was smiling at his salad and sounded more proud than critical.

"OK," I said, "I'll start tomorrow by making a detailed study of the subject."

"I know you will, but the point I am trying to make, Harry, is that we are on home turf, in New York City. Different rules apply."

"I get it, sir. I will be a ghost." The words came out on their own and made me pause. He glanced at me. But I went on, like the words had meant nothing. "I imagine it will be a McMillan TAC-50 job, either at his house or somewhere along the route."

He nodded. "I would imagine. Take a few days to study it, have a look at the route and run your plan by me before you do anything. I need to be on top of every detail, unfortunately. Not that I don't trust you, Harry. But this is New York, and I cannot pass the buck. Anything goes wrong, collateral damage, anything at all, and it's my fault."

They took the empty plates away and brought us the steaks and the *Muga*. With the wine conversation turned to Afghanistan and Iraq back in the day, when he was my commanding officer in the British SAS. We talked about surviving in the desert, men we had known like Captain Walker and the legendary Kiwi Sergeant Bradley, and eventually we came back to ghosts. I leaned back, swirling the tail end of my wine around in the glass.

"Zamudio, my Jeet Kune Do instructor, believes the ghost last night might be someone looking for revenge."

He finished his steak, wiped his mouth and dropped his napkin on the table. He signaled the waiter and said to me, "Well, that must be a pretty small pool." To the waiter he said, "Two espresso and two Macallans, no ice."

I was frowning at him. "You reckon?"

He leaned forward and spoke quietly, "Well, let's face it, Harry, they are practically all dead."

I made a doubtful face. "I hadn't thought about it like that. I guess you're right."

"Take some time tonight and think about the ones that got away, the ones who had a very high skill potential. There is also another category you haven't thought about, Harry."

"Who's that?"

"Old colleagues."

I shook my head. "No."

"Don't be sentimental. It could be SAS, SBS, SEALs or Delta, anyone you've worked with or collaborated with, and not necessarily someone with a grudge. It could be someone who has been employed to send you some kind of message, play with you or simply spook you before taking you out. Let's say a form of punishment. Either way I've posted a car on your street until this is sorted out."

I nodded. "Thanks. But if he comes again, just have them call me. I want to have a talk with this guy."

"Fine. Meanwhile, I am going to make inquiries. On the face of it, the jobs you have done which are most likely to bring reprisals are the Mohamed ben-Amini case and the Heilong Li case."

I grunted and nodded as I thought about what he was saying. "They were both representatives of huge organizations who do not like to be humiliated. His skills, and Mary Jones's status within United Chinese Petrochemicals, make China a prime candidate."

He made a face that said I hadn't seen the whole picture. "Yes, possibly, but don't forget that Mohamed ben-Amini was backed by two very powerful organizations, al-Qaeda *and* the CIA. And we are something of a thorn in the CIA's side. We have a couple of friends there, but the organization as a whole does not like us at all. They know we exist, but they do not know who we are, and they would very much like to be rid of us."

"OK, I hear you."

"So be on your toes, do the job and we'll take care of your ghost. When we find him, if it's at all feasible, we'll let you take him."

We had a couple more Macallans on the house and had the Bentley pick us up at eleven. In the car the brigadier called the guys who were watching the house and put the call on speakerphone.

"Sir."

"Have we had any visitors?"

"We been watchin' the house and we ain't seen a soul, sir."

"All right. We'll be making a delivery. Stay alert."

"You got it, sir."

Half an hour later I stood on the sidewalk and watched the Bentley pull away and turn into 5th Avenue. I climbed the steps to my front door, turned the key in the lock, went inside and closed the door. The hall was empty. The house was silent and still. I went into the living room. It was as I had left it. The kitchen was empty, quiet. I could sense nothing wrong. The ground floor was untouched and had not been visited.

I climbed the stairs with my P226 in my hand, pausing, listening as I went. All I got was that the house was empty. The second floor was clear and I climbed to the third floor where my bedroom was.

The door was open, the light was on and the drapes were closed. I had left the door closed, the lights off and the drapes open. It was blatant, a message that whoever it was could get to me whenever he wanted.

I went in, with the Sig held out in front of me. On my pillow there was a page from a newspaper. I checked the wardrobe and the en suite bathroom, but I knew already nobody was there. I holstered my pistol and went to look at the paper. The headline read: DISMEMBERED BODY FOUND BY RAIL TRACKS.

I sat on the bed and read the short article.

A DISMEMBERED, decapitated body was found in a vacant lot on Sunday, beside the railway bridge over the Major Deegan Expressway, not a hundred yards from the infamous Mescal Club. Police are working to identify the body. "It ain't easy," said Detective Harrington of the 4th Precinct, "his head and his hands have been removed, which only leaves his DNA. If he ain't in the system, were stumped."

Detectives are also checking missing persons' reports for a possible match. The victim was a middle-aged white male of approximately six feet.

THE PAPER WAS DATED 28th June, 2020.

I could remember exactly where I was that morning, and I could hazard a pretty good guess at who that body had belonged to. The only problem was, it didn't make any sense at all.

I stepped onto the landing and climbed the stairs to the attic door. The old, iron chub key was in the lock, where I always left it, but the door was unlocked. I opened it and climbed the last few steps.

The place had been empty. I'd had nothing to store up there. And the skylight had been closed. Now the skylight was open, and on the floor, against the far wall, there was a bedroll, and beside it an old-fashioned red alarm clock with two bells and a small brass hammer. I went and hunkered down beside it. That was when I saw the card lying beside the pillow. It was white and featureless, and when I opened it, it bore only the printed words, "Never send to know for whom the bell tolls..."

I am no lover of poetry, but I knew the poem by John Donne, and I knew what came next. I spoke the words softly.

"Each man's death diminishes me, for I am involved in mankind. Therefore, never send to know for whom the bell tolls; it tolls for thee."

Scan the QR code below to purchase SWEET RAZOR CUT. Or go to: righthouse.com/sweet-razor-cut

Made in United States
Orlando, FL
02 January 2026

76166233R00127